Her Relentless Cowboy

Cameron Hart

Published by Cameron Hart, 2024.

This is a work of fiction. Similarities to real people, places, or events are entirely coincidental.

HER RELENTLESS COWBOY

First edition. February 23, 2024.

Copyright © 2024 Cameron Hart.

ISBN: 979-8224637058

Written by Cameron Hart.

Want a free book?

Sign up for my newsletter[1] and get your free copy of Chasing Stacy!

One look at the stunning waitress carrying the weight of the world on her shoulders, and I'm a goner. I wasn't looking for a sweet little thing with auburn hair and more baggage than I can fit on the back of my bike, but there's no going back now. She's mine. I'll prove to her I'm more than capable of handling her past and making her feel safe again.

---

1. https://dl.bookfunnel.com/7wbqvhsx8r

Connect with me!

Check out my website, cameronhart.net[2], for sneak previews on my latest projects.

Follow me on social media:

Facebook Page - facebook.com/cameronhartauthor
Instagram - instagram.com/cameron.hart.author
TikTok - tiktok.com/@author.cameron.hart
Goodreads - goodreads.com/16081533.Cameron_Hart
Bookbub - bookbub.com/authors/cameron-hart

Chapter 1

Knox

I watch one of my oldest friends walk down the aisle with his new bride and can't help but wonder if I'll ever have what he has. Noah turned into a giant pile of mush while saying his vows to the lovely Jade. I wouldn't have believed it was possible to see the old, gruff cowboy get all choked up while declaring his undying love, but I sat in the front row and witnessed the whole thing myself.

I don't know many people at the wedding except for Noah and a few of the ranch hands here at Rivera Ranch. So when the small, intimate ceremony gives way to a much bigger reception in the newly renovated barn, I decide to grab a beer and find a wall to lean against so I can people watch.

It's nice not being the center of attention for once. Not that I'm a celebrity or anything, but I'm well known in certain circles. As a professional bull rider, I spend most of my time around other riders, fans, and the occasional groupie who is looking for a good time. I don't have many friends outside of the rodeo circuit these days, and I've never been the kind of guy to have a long-term relationship. I wouldn't say I'm a playboy by any means, but when you're a successful cowboy riding a huge fucking bull... let's just say I'm in no short supply of women who want to be with me. I don't take every one of them to bed like some other riders, but I'm only human.

Lately, however, I'm slowing down. Figuring out my priorities. Seeing Noah melt for Jade, watching the love they so clearly share, has me longing for something similar. I wouldn't have the first clue about how to be in a relationship, but if someone looked at me the way Jade looks at Noah, even from across the room, I'm pretty sure I'd move heaven and earth to make them mine. Maybe after my last ride, I can start looking for a woman of my own.

I watch as couples pair off and head to the dance floor, while others chat and make small talk with the other guests. I scoffed at the small-ass east Texas town when Noah first told me he took a gig out here four years ago. But now that I'm here, experiencing it for myself, I can see the draw. There's a true community here, something I've not been a part of in a long time.

I finish my beer and decide to find the groom and give him a hard time. My eyes sweep over the room, scanning for the tall, broad-shouldered man in a suit and a black Stetson. Noah is hard to miss, even in a crowd. He's several inches taller than everyone here except for me. I have exactly one inch on him, and I never let him forget it. I smirk to myself just thinking about all the ways I want to press his buttons and annoy him, even at his own wedding. Especially at his own wedding.

And then I see her.

Some unidentifiable thing slams into my chest and courses through my veins, hitting me so suddenly I feel like my poor heart might give out. I know with absolute certainty that my place is between her and the world. The longer I stare at her, the more this intense, all over possessive ache shifts and settles deep in my core. It's who I am now. I'm the one who will take care of her.

The beautiful woman is cutting slices of cake and handing them out to the other guests. She must be the new cook Noah said they just hired. I want to tangle my fingers in her long, silky blonde hair and smell the sweetness of her sweat after a long day of work. I want to taste, lick, nip, and worship her full pink lips, and then explore the rest of her with my tongue and fingers. More than that, I want to know why her shoulders are tense, why her smile is fake, why she won't look at anyone directly in the eyes as they thank her for the cake. I want to scoop her up in my arms and hold her until she tells me every single thing about her so I can protect her from it.

I'm vaguely aware of someone bumping into me, making me spill a bit of my beer on my boot, but I can't tear my eyes away from my woman. As if sensing me, she tips her head up, causing a few strands of her long, white-blonde hair to fall out of her updo and frame her delicate face. The way the light is slanting through the barn door and silhouetting this beautiful creature makes her look truly radiant. She darts her eyes around the room, a curious look on her face.

When her gaze falls on me, our eyes lock, and don't let go. Jesus, she's exquisite. Deep blue eyes that are almost too big for her face, but somehow fit her perfectly. She's like a precious doll that I just want to wrap up and keep all to myself. Where the hell these thoughts are coming from, I have no idea, but they are there all the same.

The more we stare at each other, the more I'm able to see. There's confusion in her eyes, along with some appreciation and curiosity. Underneath that, however, I swear I can see fear. It's as if she knows I've broken through her defenses. My angel looks down at her hands once again, depriving me of my new addiction.

I'm about to run over to her and ask what I can do to help ease her obvious anxiety, but then I see Noah. He gives Jade a sweet kiss and whispers something that makes her blush. I didn't understand any of that before, but now I know I'll be having similar sweet moments with my mystery woman. Jade heads over to the cake table, obviously sensing her new employee's distress, which puts me at ease a little bit. Jade can help her out while I gather some information from Noah. And congratulate him, of course. It is his wedding after all.

"I was starting to think we'd both be bachelors for life," I greet him with a grin.

He chuckles and shakes my hand, clapping me on the back as well for good measure. "It's good to see you, Knox. Taking some time off of the rodeo circuit?"

"I'm not a young man anymore," I sigh. "I have one last ride in a few weeks. Then I'm done."

"Wow, career change, then, huh?"

"Yeah, I might come work for you and Jade," I joke, though now that the idea is in my head, I might have to make that a reality. Anything to be closer to my woman.

"Or maybe you can get yourself a wife," he laughs. The comment is a little too on point, and I wonder how the hell he knows what I've been thinking about ever since I showed up to the wedding. "Or perhaps you're already planning to be the next one down the aisle?"

The surprise is clear in his voice, but he's not judging me. I rub the back of my neck in a nervous gesture and then finally look up at Noah. There's a weird heat creeping up my neck and into my cheeks. Shit, is this what blushing is? Am I fucking blushing over a girl? I suppose this is as good a time as any to get information out of him, so I decide to take my chances and ask about my woman.

"Actually, I, uh..." I trail off, not quite knowing what to even say. I clear my throat and try again. "Who's the new cook?"

Well, so much for subtleties. I swear Noah's eyes are going to fall right out of his head. He recovers quickly and I can tell he's choosing his next words wisely.

"Her name is Teagan," he says cautiously like he already knows I'm in too deep.

"Teagan," I say to myself, rolling her name around my tongue, swallowing it down, letting it flow through me and settle deep into the heart I wasn't sure I even had until this very moment.

"Listen, Knox. She's new here. Barely eighteen," Noah says, jarring me a bit. I mean, I knew she was young but damn. Fourteen years my junior. That should probably have me running for the hills, but instead, it has me feeling even more protective. "I don't know her story yet, none of us really do. But just...be careful."

"What do you mean? Is she in trouble? Does she need money? I have more than enough." I'm tense and practically vibrating with the need to fix everything for her until her life is as perfect as she is. I can't explain it, I just know. She's it for me.

"No, nothing like that. Jade got the sense when she did the phone interview with her that Teagan needed out of a bad situation. I don't know anything more than that, except that she's shy and a little skittish."

I might crack a tooth with how hard I'm clenching my jaw, but I can't help it. I saw with my own two eyes how shy she was, but the thought of someone making her that way, or forcing her to flee from home... Well, let's just say I know a big bad bull who would do quite a bit of damage if let loose on some unsuspecting assholes.

"All I'm saying, Knox, is to take your time. If you go after her with all this intensity that's coming off of you in waves, you're going to send her runnin' back to L.A."

I grunt in disapproval. "What the fuck was someone as precious as her doing in L.A.? That's no place for Teagan."

"See? This is exactly what I'm talking about. You're so intense. You've always been that way, you're either all in or all out."

"I'm all fucking in, Noah," I growl. Those words have never been truer than in this moment. Noah is right; once I decide on a course of action, I tend to pursue it relentlessly until I get what I want. In this case, however, it wasn't my decision. I was and am powerless to do anything but protect and provide for Teagan.

"I know, I know you are," Noah tries to calm me down. "I'm just saying—"

"Be careful. Got it," I snap at him. I know I should be congratulating him or some shit, but my entire world just tilted on its axis. "You better get back to your wife while I go *take my time* winning mine over."

Noah just chuckles, giving me a knowing look. With one last clap on the shoulder, he's off to find the love of his life. I, on the other hand, have yet to speak to mine.

Jade and Noah give each other a look full of love, and I just know they are going to be wrapped up in each other for the rest of the evening, too busy to acknowledge anyone else. I don't mind. That just means there will be more time for me to get to know Teagan.

As much as I want to run over to her and strike up a conversation, I take Noah's words into consideration. She's skittish. Shy. Probably running from something. Noah is right, my intensity would scare her away. I need to figure out how to approach her in a non-threatening way. Or, at least as non-threatening as I can be at six-foot-five and two-hundred and twenty pounds of pure muscle. Most women love the way I look, but for once I'm cursing my solid frame and towering height. The last thing on the whole goddamn planet I ever want to do is scare Teagan away.

I should probably give her space. Maybe even leave the wedding without talking to her and come back in a few days so she can get used to seeing me around the ranch.

But fuck that.

She's here right now, and I'm here, and I don't know how much longer I can go without having those ocean blue eyes on me again. Apparently, my body agrees with me, seeing as my feet are already on their way towards one of the guest tables where she's clearing off empty plates.

As I close the distance between us, I allow my eyes to wander down her slight frame. She's wearing baggy, conservative clothes, but I know she's got a killer body underneath them. I'm about to introduce myself when Teagan freezes. My large shadow falls over the table and the dishes in her hands clink together as her hands shake ever so much. Fuck, this isn't a good start.

"Hi, I'm Knox, I'm one of Noah's good friends," I introduce myself.

Teagan slowly raises her head, craning her neck up so she can meet my gaze.

Holy fuck.

She's painfully gorgeous in a way I can't even begin to understand. Now that we're this close, I can see the bags under her eyes that she's tried to conceal with makeup. No amount of makeup can take away the weary look in her eyes or the way her shoulders slump in exhaustion. Even so, she's breathtaking. Her eyelashes flutter and her brow furrows as she continues to stare at me.

"Teagan," she whispers before huffing out a breath and squeezing her eyes shut. She clears her throat and opens her eyes again. "I mean, I'm Teagan. I'm the new cook," she says with more confidence. "I'd offer to shake your hand, but mine are a bit full."

"Here, let me help." I reach out for one stack of dishes, my fingers barely grazing hers. Teagan jumps a mile high, dropping the dishes with a loud thud on the table. Luckily, none of them break since they only fell a few inches.

"I, um, I have to..."

Before she even finishes her thought, Teagan is sprinting out of the barn. Well, Noah did say she's a runner. That's okay. I know just how to rope her in.

Chapter 2

Teagan

Oh my God, oh my God, oh my GOD!

Did I seriously just freak out and run away from the hottest man in existence? Let's see...my feet are pounding the hard dirt, my arms are flailing around as if I'm trying to take flight, and one look over my shoulder confirms, that yes, I'm currently sprinting away from the Greek god with silver eyes who is staring after me like I'm some mystery to be solved.

I dart around to the other side of the barn and press my back into the wall, trying to catch my breath. For someone who ran on a treadmill for an hour every morning and evening, my real-world cardio sucks.

Or maybe it's because I was already out of breath when I started sprinting away. I couldn't help it. That man was freaking *gigantic*, a good foot or so taller than me, and good lord, those muscles. I think I might actually disappear inside of him if he tried to hug me. Then again, I wouldn't mind disappearing as long as I could be with him.

What the hell is wrong with you? Day two in your new life and you're already thinking about getting caught up in a relationship?

I take a cleansing breath and lean my head back against the wall. As much as I hate my inner monologue, this time she's right. I came here to start life on my own terms. No controlling mother, no aggressive agent, no one to monitor my daily workouts or check my calorie intake or...

No. Just. No more. I'm free from all of that. Now I just have to stay the course. I have to be the perfect employee so I can stay here and maybe even be a part of the family everyone keeps talking about. My chest gets tight when I think about belonging here the way everyone else does. I want friends who aren't just trying to use me, I want someone to look at me the way Noah looks at Jade.

But first, I have to buck up and finish my job here at the wedding. A shiver runs through me at the thought of going back into the packed reception area. I don't mind the clean up, and I loved being able to cook the meal and surprise the bride and groom with a beautiful wedding cake. It's the crowd of people I'm not a huge fan of.

I tried breathing through my anxiety like my mom taught me. I thought I was doing alright, but then the air changed. I swear it became thicker, so thick it was hard to breathe. I looked around the crowded reception area to see if anyone else was having trouble breathing, but then I saw him.

Sharp grey-green eyes, short brown hair, a strong jaw covered in just the right amount of stubble. I could tell just by looking at him that he was the kind of man who laughs and smiles a lot. I bet if I got closer, I'd even see laugh lines around his soft mouth.

But he wasn't smiling when he was looking at me. There was something else in his eyes, something... I don't know. I've never seen anyone look at me like that. With such intensity. Such purpose. The longer we stared at each other, the more I felt him winding his way around my heart and getting all tangled up in my soul.

Good thing Jade came over to save the day. I will forever be grateful that Jade gave me a chance. She's probably the first person I've ever felt completely comfortable around, and she's quickly becoming my best friend. Not that there's any competition.

After Jade left to go be all cute with her new husband, Mr. Tall, Dark, and Too Sexy for His Own Damn Good showed up. He was so much larger close up. I felt his shadow as it crept up the table and over my hands. And his voice... holy hell, like honey poured over gravel. Thick and sweet and rough. I'm ashamed to admit my lady parts started throbbing when he introduced himself. I mean, what the heck?

But it was too much. His attention, his care, the way he was stripping down all of my defenses without even trying. I felt vulnerable and shaky and my stomach started rolling. I had to get out of there before I went into full-on panic attack mode. I don't have any Xanax to calm me down this time.

My mouth grows dry and my hands shake as I bite back a wave of nausea. I don't want the long white pills. But my body does. All day I've been fighting off a massive headache and trembling limbs.

"Hey," a familiar voice booms from beside me. I jump and spin around so I'm facing the wall. The last person I want to see me have a meltdown is Knox. "Sorry, didn't mean to startle you. I wanted to see if you're okay."

I nod and press my forehead against the scratchy wood of the barn. I want to tell him I'm tired of looking over my shoulder, that I'm scared every time I close my eyes, that I'm grateful for a new start, and that I don't want to mess anything up. I want to tell him my heart is pounding, and my limbs are shaking, but I'm not sure if it's from withdrawals or just from being in his presence.

Closing my eyes, I focus on breathing. *Inhale, two, three, four. Hold, two, three, four. Exhale, two, three, four.* Again, and again I follow the breathing exercise until I feel a little bit more in control. The shaking has subsided to a slight tremor, and I don't feel like I'm going to throw up anymore, so that's a plus.

Cautiously, I turn my head to the side, pressing my cheek against the barn wall so I can get a good look at the cowboy who followed me out here. To my surprise and relief, he's not staring at me. He's leaning back on the wall, one leg crossed over the other at the ankle, arms crossed over his broad chest. Knox is looking out over the ranch and the main house. I'm grateful he isn't crowding me or gawking at me. No, he's just... here. And that's what I need right now.

After a few quiet moments of soaking up whatever peace he brought with him, I find the courage to speak.

"I'm fine," I say softly before turning around and resting my back on the wall, mirroring his stance. "I just don't like big crowds." That's not a lie. It's just not the whole truth.

Knox nods his head in understanding, glancing at me just long enough to catch my eye before going back to surveying the land. He may be comfortable with silence, but I'm sure not. I don't even know this guy and here he is, making my body go haywire and following me to remote locations.

I might just be making this up, but when he looked at me, I swear I felt like he was looking right *into* me. He probably just figured out I don't belong here. I don't belong anywhere. Shit. What if he tells Noah and Jade? I think Jade likes me enough to give me another chance, but eventually...

"Whatever it is you're thinking about over there, just let it go, angel."

I bark out a dry laugh at his little endearment. "I'm no angel, mister. Maybe a fallen one who had her wings torn off a long time ago."

Knox turns his head towards me again and I almost have to look away. He's too handsome, too intense to take in all at once. Even at a safe four or five feet away, his grey eyes sear right through me, melting my very core until I feel like I'm my entire body is one big, throbbing heartbeat.

It's more than just lust, however. He's looking at me like he did back at the reception. There's something so pure in his eyes like he's dropped all pretense and wants me to see him for who he really is. I know he's silently asking me to do the same.

"Maybe I can help you find your wings then," he whispers.

And just like that, the moment is broken. Something in me snaps. I don't know if I'm cranky from the withdrawals or if I finally reached my breaking point for assholes, but the words tumble out of my mouth before I can think twice about it.

"Let me guess, you're going to tell me that I might have left them at your place, right?" I roll my eyes and scoff. And here I thought we were connecting on some weird, intense level. Turns out he's like every other guy I've met.

"What? No, God no, I didn't mean it like..." Knox sighs and scrubs a hand down his face.

"What did you mean then?" I challenge. I don't know where this argumentative side of me is coming from. Usually, I shut up and do what I'm told. But with Knox I feel... I don't know. I feel like I could throw just about anything his way and he'd still be here for me.

"I guess that was my less than smooth way of saying I'm here for you," he says sincerely, echoing my thoughts. It's too much. Too good to be true.

"Oh yeah? You're here for me? To take care of my *needs* day or night?"

"Jesus, woman, is sex all you think about?" he says, throwing up his hands in frustration.

"Me? What about you? Sending me those looks at the reception and then following me out here. I'm not going to give you a show or follow you back to your place. I'm not easy prey, I'm not a toy, and I don't care what you think you can do for my career! I'm not a whore, I never even wanted this!" I yell. I'm shaking again, and so lightheaded I feel like I might pass out.

Knox takes a tentative step towards me, and for some reason, I don't move away. He reaches a hand out and I flinch on instinct, slamming my eyes shut and tucking my head into my shoulder.

Then I feel warm, calloused fingertips brush across my temple and down the side of my face, where Knox tucks some of my hair behind my ear. His touch is achingly tender. I want to beg him for more, but I also want to go hide under a blanket and pretend this whole day never happened.

"I don't know who you were talking to, angel, but I'm not that guy. I'm not going to hurt you. I'm not going to use you. All I want is to take care of you."

I open my eyes and see only kindness and concern. Why does that make me want to cry? Dammit! I'm made of stronger stuff than this. I didn't survive a lifetime of bullshit and then come all the way out here just to fall into another trap!

I gather up all the courage I can muster and step away from the gorgeous, too-nice stranger. "I don't need anyone to take care of me, thanks," I say in my most professional voice. I am still at work, after all.

Spinning around on my foot, I take off towards the front of the barn so I can continue cleaning up the guest tables and cut more cake if necessary. I get about five feet away when my left foot hits a big rock at a weird angle, and I go tumbling down. I bite back a yelp and try to land as gracefully as I can.

Knox is by my side in a second.

"Teagan, are you okay?"

God, hearing him say my name in his stupidly sexy voice shouldn't be such a turn on.

"Mmhmm," I mumble while sitting up and then trying to get to my feet. My left ankle buckles a bit, and he steadies me by throwing an arm around my waist and tucking me into his side. I take a moment to breathe him in - leather and grass and citrus. It's light and earthy and perfect. His warmth seeps into my skin and I allow myself one more second to feel cherished in his strong embrace. Pushing myself off of his chest, I take a few tentative steps on my own.

"See? I told you I don't need your—"

And then a sharp pain shoots up my leg and I go down. Hard.

"Teagan!" Knox bellows, even though he's only a few feet away. He scoops me up in my arms and holds me close, looking down at me with equal parts concern and annoyance. That's fair. I'm being a brat and I know it.

"I'm really quite fine. If walking around in six-inch heels taught me anything, it's how to take care of a twisted ankle," I deadpan.

"Why were you walking around in six-inch heels?" he asks, standing in place with me in his arms. It's kind of ridiculous. And sweet.

I shrug, not wanting to give too much myself away just yet. Or ever. Yes, let's go with never, ever talking about anything that happened before coming here. Knox looks like he wants to say something but decides against it. Good man.

"I just need some ice, which we have plenty of at the reception. So, if you could just set me down…" I trail off, waiting for him to realize he's still holding me. Instead, he squeezes me tighter.

Ugh, what is it about this man? He's so sweet I want to kick him.

I give him my best scowl, but Knox looks down at me and grins. Like… wow. Sparkling eyes, straight white teeth, dimples and everything.

"Might want to wait till your ankle heals before you go around kicking me," he drawls.

Oh crap, did I say that out loud? I feel my face burning up as he continues to grin at me. I bury my face in my hands, but Knox leans down and kisses them, making me swoon despite my best efforts.

"The sweeter you are, the harder I'm going to kick you, you know," I warn.

Knox smiles, grazing his lips along my forehead and cheek, finally landing on the shell of my ear.

"That's what I'm counting on," he whispers.

Oh fuck.

I think… I think my panties are wet. And I think I need to get out of his arms before I do something stupid like make him give me my first kiss.

As if sensing the turn in my feelings, Knox simply presses a kiss to my forehead and then starts walking me towards my cabin.

"Um, hello? Not my cabin, you giant lug of a cowboy, the reception!"

Knox chuckles, a deep, rich sound that rumbles from his chest to mine. "You got a busted-up ankle, love. You're not working right now, we gotta take care of you."

"Not working?" Panic runs through me. Of course I messed up already. What was I thinking trying to have a new life somewhere far away? "I don't know what it is that you do, *Knox*, but I just got this job and I'm expected to be here to help tear everything down. Now, please turn this car around and take me back to the reception."

"Calm down, Teagan. You can—"

"When, in the history of the entire world, has telling someone to *calm down* actually helped them calm down?"

Knox takes a deep breath and stops walking for a moment. "You're right. You have the right to feel however you want to feel." The sincerity behind his words has me hiding my tears behind a glare. "I was just trying to tell you that you don't have to worry about your job. Most people are heading out, the ranch hands and I can tear it all down, and you are hurt. Jade and Noah would agree that you need to rest up."

I furrow my brow. "Rest up? For how long? I'm really okay. Knox, I need this job. Please don't tell Jade and Noah that I already screwed up." His eyes go soft at my admission. I don't like being this vulnerable.

"You didn't screw up. It was an accident; anyone can see that. But you do have to take care of yourself. There's no sense in risking your health just to get a few hours of work in, right?"

My throat closes and my eyes well up with tears. Is he serious? He just wants me to be... healthy? To put my job second? These are all foreign concepts to me, but the rich comfort of his voice, the steady beat of his heart, and the way he's looking at me right now... I believe him. Instead of crying, I cross my arms and turn away from him, like a little kid throwing a temper tantrum. Okay, so maybe I let one tear slip. Knox does his best not to notice.

"You have people who care now. All you have to do is let us." He says it so quietly I almost don't hear him.

When we're finally standing on my porch, Knox sets me down on the ground. I want to thank him, not only for carrying me but for being my punching bag and also for being nice to me even though I've been a big brat. Instead, I mouth off to him.

"Worst Uber ride ever. Made me cry and took me to the wrong place."

Knox laughs so hard he has to grab onto the railing to hold himself upright. This makes me smile too, like a real, actual smile. I didn't think I was capable of those anymore.

"My apologies, Teagan. Can I make it up to you by wrapping your ankle up in ice and getting you some hot tea?"

I raise a dubious eyebrow and cross my arms over my chest. "You almost had me there, Knox. But no, you can't come in."

He puts his hands up in surrender. "I promise I won't try anything else. I just want to—"

"Take care of me, yeah, I got it." What I don't say is that it's not *him* I'm worried about. It's me. I think I might jump his freaking bones even if I have no clue how to do that.

Knox shakes his head and tsks at me playfully. "So cynical. That's okay though. I've always enjoyed a challenge. I'll take care of you, love, one way or another."

I burst out laughing while Knox groans and dips his head down in defeat.

"I swear I didn't mean for that to come out as a threat!"

I laugh again and shake my head. "I know. I think you're the least subtle person I've ever met. If you wanted to threaten me, you'd just come right out and do it." I meant it as another joke, but his eyes grow serious.

"I'm not threatening you, Teagan. Not now, not ever. I want you to trust me."

Be still my heart and calm the fuck down, my ovaries.

"I think I'd like that," I whisper.

Knox tucks my hair behind my ear again and kisses my forehead. He tips his cowboy hat at me and turns around without another word.

Holy hell. I'm in so much trouble.

Chapter 3

Knox

"That's it, Teagan, fuck, just like that," I groan, gripping her hair and guiding her hot little mouth over my cock. Up and down she goes, taking a little more of me each time until I reach the back of her throat. She moans, sending vibrations up my cock and deep into my core.

I buck my hips, causing Teagan to choke on my dick. I growl and do it again, loving her sloppy wet sounds as she sucks me off. Her soft pink tongue laps at the vein on the underside of my cock, making the fucker jerk and leak inside of her mouth.

"Mmphmm," Teagan mumbles with a mouth full of me. God fucking damn, this woman has me ready to go off.

I cup her face in both of my hands and fuck her pretty little mouth, loving the way she submits to me, letting me take my pleasure, knowing I'm going to give it all back to her and then some.

"Fuck, fuck, fuck!" I yell as the first tremor of my orgasm shoots down my spine and out of my aching shaft. Teagan moans and swallows me down, rope after rope of my sticky seed coating her mouth as she licks and massages more out of me. One last burst of cum leaves my cock, and then...

"Holy shit," I grumble, throwing my blankets off my sweaty body and taking my cock in my hand. Two rough strokes are all it takes for me to erupt into my hand and throw my head back in ecstasy. Jesus.

I've woken up to filthy thoughts of my sweet and sassy Teagan every morning now for a whole goddamn week. I wanted to give her space, give her time to get settled into her new responsibilities at the ranch, but I don't know how much longer I can stay away.

I've rubbed my dick raw the last seven days, and still, I know the only true cure will be burying myself deep inside of her creamy cunt once and for all. It's not just sex I want from her, though I know it's going to be incredible and life changing. It's everything. I meant what I told her at the wedding; I want to take care of her in every single way.

Holding her in my arms, even though she was fighting me every step of the way—literally—triggered some primal instinct in me to haul her off and claim her so the whole fucking world would know she's mine and I'm hers.

But I knew I was coming on too strong. I think we ended things on a good note, but good god, the woman has walls a mile high. I was glad to see some fight in her, even if it was directed at me. Noah said she was shy and skittish, and while I saw a bit of that, I loved the moment she chose to snap at me. I can take whatever fight she has as long as it's me she's fighting with.

I'll do whatever it takes to prove to her she can trust me, that I'm not just using her. White-hot anger burns through me at the mere thought of her words from that day. She started off yelling at me, and then somewhere in the middle her anger grew into something else entirely. It was like she was yelling at her past and everyone who ever wronged her. I want to yell at them too. I want to do far more than yell, in fact. But that will come later.

For now, I need to be around her again.

***

Four hours later, I'm sitting in Jade and Noah's office in the main house of Rivera Ranch, sipping sweet tea and trying to talk my way into a seasonal job.

"I thought you were kidding when you said you might come work for us," Noah says, looking at me with equal parts doubt and amusement.

"I'll admit, maybe at the time it was a joke, but now I'm serious. You don't need to pay me, lord knows I don't have a cash flow problem, and I can take your old cabin, Noah, since you're up here in the main house now. Or, hell, put one of the other guys in your cabin and let me bunk in their bed instead. I don't care, I just want to be here. Need it, actually."

"I'm sorry, I think I missed something," Jade cuts in, bouncing her eyes between Noah and me.

"Knox here is in love with Teagan," Noah supplies dryly.

"Really?!" Jade perks up, a smile lighting up her face.

I nod and grin like a fool. "Yes, ma'am. I'm going to make her my wife one of these days, but for now, I just need to be around her. You can understand that, can't you?"

Noah opens his mouth, but Jade claps her hand over it. Noah gives her a stern look but Jade just rolls her eyes and giggles. God, he's so whipped by the little lady. I can't wait to be the same for my angel.

"Can I get you a refill?" Jade asks sweetly. I nod, even though I don't really want a refill. I get the sense she needs the excuse to go back to the kitchen. "Great. Noah, want to help me?"

I chuckle at the big oaf following Jade down the stairs like an obedient puppy. I'm pretty sure my plan is going to work out, but even if it doesn't, I'll find another way to be around Teagan.

My hands itch to hold her again, to feel the weight of her in my arms, her warmth against my chest. I felt her hip bone dig into my stomach when I carried her, and the individual bones in her spine as I held her tiny body. It angers me to think that she had to go without food for any reason. My angel is perfect, but I want to hand feed her every meal to make sure she never goes hungry again.

I only have fragments of her life before the ranch. I've gathered all of them up in my mind this last week and tried to line them up and make some sort of bigger picture out of them. Six-inch heels. Not enough food. Cynical. Afraid of human touch, at least at first. My heart clenches up painfully, remembering the way she flinched when I reached out to tuck her hair behind her ear. Goddamn, I want to punch any motherfucker who dared to put his hands on her.

"See?" Noah whisper to Jade. "The dude looks like he's gonna blow a gasket, and that's the last thing Teagan, or hell, any of us needs."

I open my eyes, not even realizing I had squeezed them shut. I unclench my fists and take a deep breath as I roll my shoulders out.

Jade and Noah are standing in the doorway, staring at me while bickering back and forth. Finally, I stand up and hold my hands out in front of me in a sign of surrender. It's an odd and unnatural state of being for me, but I'll do anything for my angel.

"I know I'm intense, as you like to remind me, Noah, but I swear to you it's only out of this insane need to protect Teagan. Fuck, I... Just thinking about someone hurting her or starving her, I—"

"Starving her?" Jade gasps.

"I mean, I don't know her story for sure, I just know I could feel her bones when I carried her back to the cabin after she twisted her ankle."

"She twisted her ankle?" Noah grits out, looking over to Jade to see if she knew about this. One shake of her head lets him know she had no idea.

"Damn stubborn woman," I mutter. "She didn't tell you? Was she icing it? Putting her foot up?"

The look Jade and Noah share tells me everything I need to know. I sigh and run my fingers through my short hair, trying to keep my shit together. I know Teagan isn't used to people worrying about her, but Jesus, she has to take care of herself. And if she won't, then I will.

"Maybe Knox is right, he could be good for her. Watch out for her and such," Jade says thoughtfully. I'm nodding my head a little too eagerly at her tentative support.

Noah gives me a hard stare. I want to be upset with him for keeping me from my woman, but I find I'm thankful that Teagan has people on her side who want the best for her, even if she doesn't know it.

"If you're staying on the land and working as a ranch hand, you *will* be working. You can't just follow Teagan around like a creep. You'll do your fair share, just like the rest of us," Noah informs me. I try to hide my grin, knowing that he's about to agree to let me stay on.

"Of course. You've known me since I was practically a kid when we worked on our first ranch together. I learned from the best, boss," I wink. Noah just grunts, but I see him hiding a smile. Noah took me, the new, scrawny kid, under his wing and never once made me feel dumb when I messed up. He truly was and is the best friend I've ever had, and I know he can see my true intentions, even if he's giving me a hard time.

"What about the rest of your riding career? Are you willing to give that up for life on the ranch again?" Noah asks.

"Like I told you before, I just have one ride left, and not for another six weeks. Just let me work here at least until then. When I'm done with my last ride, we can talk about a longer-term arrangement. I'm hoping to have Teagan as my bride not long after that, but if she needs more time, I'll respect that."

Neither Jade nor Noah bat an eye at my timeline. These two fell in love and got married in about that same amount of time. With one final look, Jade nods her head and holds out her hand for me to shake.

"Welcome aboard, Knox," she says, giving me a firm handshake. She doesn't let go, however. Instead, Jade squeezes my hand with a surprising amount of force. I tick my eyes over to Noah, who has a smirk on his face. "If you upset Teagan in any way, if you betray her or hurt her, I will end you."

Hot damn, the look in her eyes leaves no room for doubt. I believe this little slip of a woman would murder me in my sleep and then order the other ranch hands to cut me up and bury my pieces all over the ranch.

"Understood," I say, giving her another firm handshake.

"Great!" Jade claps her hands as if she didn't just threaten to kill me. "Go get your stuff moved into Noah's old cabin. You start tomorrow, bright and early."

We say our goodbyes and I head downstairs. I'm almost to the front door when I hear soft humming coming from the kitchen. My heart stills in my chest and then kicks into high gear. All of the hair on the back of my neck stands up as a shiver runs down my spine. It's Teagan. I know before I even turn around.

Slowly, I shuffle my way towards her voice, which is angelic like the rest of her. I stand back and to the left of the open kitchen, to where I can see her but am easily hidden by the China cabinet.

My Teagan is in tight jeans, a baggy t-shirt, and an apron. Her blonde hair is piled on top of her head, and she swipes a hand across her forehead, leaving a little smear of flour there. I long to wipe it off, but that will have to wait. The sudden image of Teagan in an apron and nothing else flashes through my head. I'd bend her over the counter and eat out her juicy little pussy before slamming my cock deep inside, hitting places she didn't even know she had.

Fuck.

I bite down on my bottom lip to keep my groan at bay and then swallow down my lustful thoughts. Teagan's hips sway back and forth to the rhythm of whatever song she's humming, each movement mesmerizing me and pulling me deeper under her spell. When she's done mixing whatever is in the bowl, Teagan dips her finger in and licks off a bit of the batter.

God. Damn.

I want her lips wrapped around my dick, just like my dream this morning. My dirty thoughts turn tender when I see the soft smile play across her lips. Teagan sighs and tips her head back like she's trying to freeze this moment in her mind. I'm doing the same. I want to remember how peaceful and content she looks in this moment with the sun tangling in her white-blonde hair, her creamy skin kissed by the rays of light, her eyes closed in complete serenity. I'm going to make sure she looks this content every single day for the rest of her life.

Before I either get caught or get a raging hard-on, I turn on my heel and walk away. I've got to pack up and move in, after all. I'll rest easier tonight knowing I'll be able to keep a closer eye on my angel starting tomorrow.

Chapter 4

Teagan

Don't lie to me, you selfish bitch! I called in a million favors to get you" *this gig, and now you're risking it all for what? A donut? A taco? What* *"?did you eat? What gave you that pimple*

"!Nothing! It just happens sometimes, people get pimples, Mom"

Not you. Pimples mean grease, which means fat, which means you've" *been eating something not in your diet plan," my mom spits out, scrolling* *through her phone to check my latest entry on the meal planning app we* *.both have*

"..I don't think that's exactly how pimples work"

You're not paid to think. You're paid to look pretty. I know you're" *lying to me, Teagan. Tell me what you ate, and I won't make you throw* *"up*

?What?!" Is she fucking insane"

You heard me. What was it? Did your tutor order pizza for you? I" *"thought after I fired that last one, the others would take note*

"—No, I'm sticking to the plan, I'm just stressed"

Oh, you're stressed? Think about how much more stressed out you'd be" *if we were broke! That's exactly what's going to happen if you put on more* *weight and get pimples. This isn't about some fleeting indulgence, Teagan.* *".This is about your career*

.I'm sixteen, sometimes I just get pimples," I mumble under my breath"

The next thing I know, my mom grabs my arm and drags me into the *small bathroom in my dressing room. She twists it behind my back and* *kneels down on the floor, forcing me to do the same. She pins me up against* *the toilet, one hand in my hair and the other one around my neck.*

".Throw up"

"?What"

You heard me. You have to get the toxic sugars and fats out of your" *"system right now before they do any more damage*

I'm about to argue with her about how inaccurate all of that is, but now doesn't seem like the best time.

"—Mom, I"

Enough. You want to eat whatever you want? Then I'll make you" "throw it up

Before I can say or do anything else, my mom tightens her grip on my hair and moves her other hand from my throat to my mouth, sticking two fingers inside. I gag and sputter and try to twist away from her. Unfortunately, she's got about a hundred pounds on me. For all her talk about no sugar or fats, my mom gets to eat whatever she wants.

I don't like doing this, Teagan. But I'll do whatever is necessary to" help you reach your career goals. Get yourself cleaned up. The shoot starts "in an hour

I wake up in a cold sweat and race towards the bathroom. I'm not sure if my stomach is turning because of my nightmare or because of my withdrawals. I've been doing better the last few days. I hope the worst of it is over. I'd be absolutely mortified if anyone found out I had a bit of a pill problem. It's all part of my old life, and once I get the shakes and nausea under control, that part of me will be over and done with for good.

Thankfully I'm able to take a few deep breaths and calm down. After a cool shower and some deep breathing exercises, I feel a little more at ease.

The clock on my nightstand reads three fifteen in the morning. I groan, knowing my alarm is going to go off in fifteen minutes. There's not much I miss about my old life. In fact, there's just one thing - sleeping in. Waking up at three-thirty for the last week has been rough, but I'm glad to make that sacrifice if it means I get to cook and be a part of the family here.

I laugh softly to myself as I get dressed for the day. Me. A cook. My mom would absolutely *die*. I'll admit, I'm okay with that. Over the years, I got really good at creating recipes that both fit within my mom's guidelines *and* tasted pretty good. I had to get creative with substitutions, and while a lot of my first meals and snacks were a huge swing and a miss, I managed to learn from my mistakes.

My entire world opened up when Jade called and offered me this job. I immediately began searching for recipes that included real butter, sugar, and **gasp** carbs! I'm still trying to find my own personal style and flavor, but I think I've done a good job feeding everyone in the meantime.

I grab the key to the main house and my notebook full of recipe ideas and head over to the main house. I'm about thirty minutes earlier than I normally am, but that just gives me more time to try out a new recipe. I'm thinking a maple bacon French toast casserole. If it sucks, then I'll still be able to fix up something quick like omelets...

I stop short when I see a large figure looming on the back porch, right by the door to the kitchen. Fear grips my lungs and my legs turn to lead. The only thing I can hear is the beat of my heart as it thrashes around in my chest.

It can't be Mom. She's a large lady, but she's not that tall. Or broad. Or muscled...

Everything in me relaxes, almost to the point of falling over. It's Knox. I can only see his silhouette, but I know it's him. Now my heart is thrashing around for a whole new reason.

"Is this you officially threatening me?" I ask as I approach the sexy, strong cowboy who has taken up far too many of my thoughts this last week.

Knox kicks off from where he was leaning against the house and chuckles. It's a deep, scratchy sound, like maybe he's not used to being up this early either.

"Already told you, angel, I'm no threat. I'm just here for an honest days' work and a good meal." Knox smiles at me as I approach and winks. Damn him and his beautiful grey eyes and dimples.

"And I told *you*, I'm no angel," I say once I get the door unlocked.

"Right. You're a ninja. Wanting to kick me and all just for being nice," he teases.

I roll my eyes and flip on the lights in the kitchen, beelining towards the coffee maker.

"Speaking of," Knox continues, following me right in as if he owns the place. "How's your ankle? Did you ice it? Rest up? Take some pain pills?"

"What?" I say a little too forcefully. "I mean, it's fine. I'm fine."

Real smooth, idiot. At least it's better than yelling at him to shove his stupid pain pills up his ass.

"Everything okay?"

"Yes," I snap. "I just told you that. I'm fine. My ankle is fine. Everyone and everything is fine. I just have a headache," I add, hoping to give him some reasonable explanation for my mood swings. Plus, it's not a lie. I've had a headache for days.

"I'm sure there's some Aspirin in the bathroom down the hall, let me grab it for you," Knox offers reasonably. Some part of me knows he doesn't mean anything by it, and that Aspirin is non-habit forming, but it's all hitting a little too close to home for me to think rationally.

"Stop trying to feed me pills, I said I'm fucking fine," I grit out. I watch Knox's eyes go from concerned to confused to shocked, and then back to concerned.

I didn't realize my hands started shaking until I feel Knox's large, warm, calloused hands cover mine so tenderly.

"Take a breath for me, Teagan. I'm not trying to feed you pills, I just don't want you to be in pain," he tells me softly like I'm some rabid animal.

I open my mouth to either berate him or apologize, I haven't decided which yet, but then I'm gut-punched by the sudden urge to throw up. Yanking my hands away from his, I dash down the hall to the bathroom and lean over the toilet. Since I haven't eaten in nearly ten hours, I only dry heave.

Knox is on me in a flash, gathering my hair and holding it back, taking care of me just like he keeps promising me he will.

I can't. Just. Fucking. Can't.

He rubs my back while I sob into the toilet. I hate that he's seeing me like this, but it's probably for the best. There's no way he could be attracted to me after witnessing this hot mess.

When I'm all cried out, Knox carefully leans me back against the bathroom wall and grabs a washcloth. He gets it wet with cool water and wipes my tears away before folding the cloth up and placing it on the back of my neck. It feels refreshing and is surprisingly calming. I'll have to remember that for next time.

"Now, are you going to tell me what's really going on?" he asks as he gets himself situated next to me. Knox is sitting on the floor, leaning against the wall, with his elbows resting on his bent knees. I'd laugh at the huge man trying to fold himself in beside me, but I'm still on the verge of tears and I feel like I might have a complete meltdown if I let out any emotion at all.

I open my mouth to say...something. I'm not sure what. The truth? An elaborate story? Possibly telling him to mind his own business? I close my mouth, take a breath, and try again. Only nothing comes out.

"Take your time," he whispers.

Something about that tugs at my heart. I turn towards him and rest my forehead on his large bicep. Knox doesn't make a move to pull me closer or push me away, sensing that this is all I can handle right now.

"My mom signed me up for a commercial audition when I was five," I begin, wanting to be honest with him. Hell, it's the first time I've been honest with anyone, the first time anyone cared enough to stick around for my story. "I got the gig. One commercial led to another and another. Eventually, Mom got me an agent who wanted to try my talent at modeling. From there things sort of...spiraled, I guess."

"Spiraled, how?" Knox asks quietly after I've been silent for a few moments.

I shrug, trying to find the right words. "I did ads for kid's clothing lines for a while and then when I hit puberty, mom wanted me to do bigger ticket gigs. She pulled me out of school and made sure I had tutors so I could get my schoolwork done in between photo shoots and auditions. She and my agent, Oscar, got more and more controlling. I had a strict diet and exercise regimen to follow. Every calorie was monitored and when I ate something bad..." I blow out a breath and take a second to compose myself. "When I ate something bad, my mom would make me throw up."

"Jesus," Knox grunts.

"I started getting panic attacks before photoshoots because that seemed to be when my mom was the most paranoid about my diet. She started giving me these pills when I was fifteen. She said her doctor prescribed them to help with anxiety. I started taking one before going on set, and then two, and then...I don't know. I just took however many made it all go away. I felt numb and groggy and honestly, most of that time feels like a blur. My mom always had the pills on her and when I got argumentative or had an opinion about something, she'd toss me a bottle of Xanax, knowing I'd eventually take the pills and chill out."

I fill my lungs with air before continuing. "I knew things were getting out of control. I wanted to stop with the pills and try life without them. She agreed after a big fight, but I found her crushing up the pills in my breakfast smoothie the week after. That's when I knew I had to get out. I started applying to jobs, knowing I'd be turning eighteen soon, and well...here I am."

By the time I get it all off my chest, I realize I somehow ended up practically sitting in Knox's lap. He's got one big arm around my back, holding me close to his side, and I have one arm draped over his stomach. Yes, he has perfectly sculpted abs. Because of course he does.

"And you quit the Xanax cold turkey, huh?" he asks, connecting the dots between what I told him and the shitshow of a morning I've had. I nod and bury my face into his chest, breathing in leather and grass and citrus. His smell is already familiar and comforting.

"It's been ten days. I did some research, the worst of it should be over soon. I...Knox, please don't tell anyone. I don't want them to think I'm some...some..."

"Some strong, brave, badass?" he finishes for me, squeezing me tightly before loosening his grip a bit.

"I'm not brave," I whisper. "I'm afraid. All the time," I tell him truthfully.

"Being brave doesn't mean you're not afraid. In fact, most of the time it means you're scared shitless. And then you do the damn thing anyway."

This makes me laugh and then sniffle a bit into his chest, no doubt getting his shirt all snotty and wet in the process. Knox drops a kiss on top of my head, which makes me sigh contentedly. I guess it's kind of nice letting someone take care of me for a little while.

"Take it from me," Knox continues as he untangles himself from me. "I go toe to toe with bulls for a living."

"You're a bull rider? Like, for real?" I ask, caught totally off guard.

"Yup," he confirms, getting to his feet and holding out his hand for me. "I'll tell you all about it while we cook some breakfast." He winks at me, giving me that heart-stopping grin of his. This time, I return it with one of my own.

Before I know it, Knox and I are in the kitchen, working on breakfast like we've done it every morning for years. I won't lie, something about that calms me deep inside. I feel a peace that I haven't felt in...well, I don't think I've ever felt this way.

"So, you're a hotshot bull riding chef who likes to slum it on the ranch with us regular folk?" I tease.

"Careful now, angel. Wouldn't want me to tell Noah or Jade that you think Rivera Ranch is *slumming it*."

I roll my eyes and bump him with my hip. Knox bumps me back, making me giggle. God, how can he make me laugh after I just spilled my guts to him? I've laughed and smiled more around Knox the two times I've met him than I have the last ten years of my life.

"I'm no hotshot, but I've been working the rodeo circuit ever since I was a kid. Before going pro, I was a ranch hand. That's how Noah and I met, actually."

"Wait, which is it? Are you working here or are you a rodeo star?"

Knox chuckles and flips the bacon while I work on chopping up veggies for the omelets. I took too long bawling in the bathroom to make the French toast casserole, but I'm not mad about how things turned out.

"Not a rodeo star," he emphasizes again. "And yes, I'm working here for the time being. At least five weeks, until the final ride of my career. This bull and I have a history, and I can't wait to put him in his place."

"You *are* a rodeo star!" I say with an exaggerated gasp.

"There's my sassy girl," Knox says with all of the affection in the world. There go my heart and my ovaries again. He's too freaking kind and sexy for his own good. I'm practically swooning over here, which is not something I do. Ever. But who could blame me?

I laugh and grab the eggs, scrambling them in a big bowl and adding some milk and butter. "What's the story behind the bull? Is he a mean motherfucker? You need backup? I'll get some of those cute cowgirl boots with spurs and a lasso with spikes on it. Do those exist? If not, they should."

"As much as I want to see you lasso a bull, love, I need to take this one on myself. I've gotta end my career on a high note and make sure that bull knows who's boss."

Knox winks as he tells me this, but his smile is tight. There's a fierceness to his features that makes me wonder what his real motivation is. Who is he trying to prove himself to?

"Is it dangerous?" I ask, suddenly afraid of losing him. Not that he's *mine* to lose, per se. But I just told him things I've never told anyone before and now I'm starting to feel things I've never felt before.

Knox laughs at my question, and this time his smile is genuine. I know I've barely spent more than a few hours with the man, but I swear I know him, feel him all the way down to my bones.

"Nothing I can't handle. I'm a rodeo star, after all."

I stick my tongue out at him and toss a chunk of diced green pepper his way. It bounces off his chest, and for some reason that makes me want to tear his shirt off and lick those defined muscles.

Reel it in, woman!

He gets a mischievous look in his eyes, and yup, my panties are practically ruined. Damn him. Knox opens his mouth to say something, but just then, the backdoor swings open. Cody, Zane, and Jacob shuffle inside, followed by Isaiah.

Knox leans in close to me and whispers, "I'll get you back for that, angel."

"Is that a threat?" I ask, raising one eyebrow in challenge.

Knox just grins and winks at me before taking the plate of bacon over to the table and introducing himself to the guys.

I'm in trouble alright. And I think I like it.

Chapter 5

Knox

It's been three weeks since I started working at the ranch. Three weeks since Teagan let her walls down just enough to talk to me. Three weeks since I held her while she cried. I had hoped to have my ring on her finger and my baby in her belly by now, but after all the shit she's been through, I knew I needed to take my time.

I still can't believe my angel has been through so much. Her entire life she's been surrounded by people who want to use her for their own selfish purposes. Her own fucking mother starving her, making her throw up, and encouraging a drug habit for Christ's sake. How can one human do that to another human, let alone their own child?

Teagan is stronger than all of that, though. She's a warrior, that much is clear. Not only did she survive her messed up childhood, but she was suffering through detox on her own, too ashamed to ask for help. I don't blame her; I'm sure I'd have all sorts of trust issues if I were in her position, but it hurt knowing I could have been there for her sooner if only I had known.

Since that day, I've spent as much time with her as I can without crowding her or neglecting my responsibilities on the ranch. We cook breakfast together most mornings, and I even convinced her to do her grocery shopping on Tuesdays, which are my day off, so I can go with her.

My angel still has her demons, and she still struggles with anxiety and tremors from the withdrawals, but she's getting stronger all the time. I thought maybe Teagan would be shy about eating, but to my delight, she *loves* food. She's putting meat on her bones and getting healthier and happier with each passing day. There's more light than dark in her eyes, and while I know a lot of that has to do with being here on the ranch, I'd like to think I contributed to it as well.

The ranch has been good for me, too. I may have started out working here to be closer to Teagan, but I can't deny the sense of accomplishment and satisfaction I've had since starting my new job. It feels damn good to work with my hands again, to problem solve, and hell, to shoot the shit with the guys.

I have friends from the rodeo circuit, but I've come to realize those friendships were shallow at best and manipulative at worst. No one has contacted me in the month I've been away, and that's just fine by me. Out of sight out of mind. But the guys here - Jacob, Isaiah, Cory, and Zane, they are solid. When you're working side by side with someone for twelve hours a day, you tend to form strong bonds. Like Noah and me. I didn't realize how much I've missed that kind of connection in my life.

It certainly makes leaving the rodeo easier. I'll get my last ride in, finish my career on a high note, tie up loose ends, and then Teagan and I will start on our forever. I know Teagan is worried about me going back to the rodeo, but I'll prove to her I'm not a man who is easily defeated. I'll prove it to everyone.

"How's life on the ranch treating you?" Noah asks me as we head up to the main house for dinner.

"I've missed it," I tell him truthfully.

Noah gives me a skeptical look. "I'll be honest, I thought you'd slack off or give up after the first week. But I gotta say, you've pulled your weight around here."

"You wound me, old friend!" I say dramatically while clapping a hand over my heart as if in pain. "You of all people should know I'm made of stronger stuff than that."

"Knox, it's been over a decade since you've done work like this. I just assumed you were living the high life, soaking up the glory and doing jack shit," he jokes.

"Hey now! I do...things," I defend lamely. Noah chuckles and shakes his head. "Being out here, getting my hands in the dirt, bonding with the guys...it's all been really eye-opening."

Noah and I walk in silence for a bit. He's never been one to press the issue, which in turn makes me want to tell him more. He's good for me like that.

I finally break after a few minutes, ignoring the smug smirk on his face like he knows just what he's doing.

"I thought maybe being a successful bull rider would be my peak, you know? I could have ridden that ol' son of a bitch bull at the beginning of the summer, but I pushed it back. It's not that I'm afraid of the bull, more just...what happens after my eight seconds are up? But these last few weeks have shown me there really is life after the rodeo. I almost wish I didn't have the stupid ride hanging over my head so I could go ahead and get started on the rest of my life."

"So then why do it? Are you under contract or something?"

"Nah," I shake my head. "This one is personal. It's..." I trail off, not quite sure how to put it into words what this represents to me.

We've reached the porch, but neither one of us makes a move to go inside. Instead, we're leaning against the railing pretending not to have a heart-to-heart. We're fuckin' cowboys, after all. I spit in the dirt for good measure.

"It's about Anthony, isn't it?" Noah finally asks.

I shrug and look out over the ranch, following the expanse of land with my eyes as it stretches out to kiss the sky. "Like I said. It's personal."

"I don't think he ever meant for it to take over your life. He wanted you to be happy, and now you have a chance at that with Teagan. Don't fuck it up because of some misplaced—"

"You don't get it," I bite out, clenching my fists at my sides. "It's not what you think. There's...he..."

"Look, Knox, you don't have to tell me shit. But you do owe Teagan an explanation. Jade kept stuff from me that ultimately put her in danger. We worked through it, and I thank God every day she's here with me, safe and happy and healthy. I wouldn't wish that kind of hurt or anxiety on anyone, let alone my oldest friend."

"Don't get all sappy on me, old man," I grumble, going for a joke but not quite hitting the tone right. I force the tension to roll off my shoulders with a sigh.

"I'm serious. Jade threatened to murder you if you hurt Teagan, but here's my official warning. Talk to her. Tell her your shit. Don't let it come between you. If you lose your girl over something as stupid as keeping the truth from her, I promise that being drawn and quartered by Jade will be a welcome distraction from the inner turmoil you'll carry around with you."

"Well, damn. I guess that's that then, huh?"

"There you two are!" Jade swings the door open and wraps her arms around Noah before he has a chance to say anything else. The tough, no bullshit rancher softens the instant he looks at Jade. "Come on, Teagan has a delicious dinner waiting for us, you two can braid each other's hair and gossip later."

Noah pinches Jade, who squeals and scampers back inside the house.

"Think about what I said," Noah tells me before following his wife inside.

I take a minute to compose myself and head into the kitchen myself. I'm greeted with the sight of my beautiful angel wiping her hands on her apron and untying it from her tiny waist. She tucks a strand of her light blonde hair behind her ears and looks up at me.

Jesus, every single time her eyes meet mine I have to remember how to breathe. Those deep blue eyes twinkle as she smiles at me, her cheeks dusted with the faintest hue of pink. I don't know how much longer I can keep my hands off her. All I want to do is stride over and pull her into me so I can claim her lips once and for all.

But Noah is right, damn him. I don't want to take things to the next level without telling her everything about me. She already opened up about her past, so of course she deserves for me to do the same.

Dinner is torture, just like it is every night. Not because of the food, of course. Teagan is an excellent cook, and she knows just how to make hearty, classic dishes with a bit of a healthy twist that everyone loves. There's plenty of dessert too, to balance out the healthier meals, of course.

No, dinner is torture because I don't want to share Teagan with anyone. I want all of her smiles, all of her words, all of her laughter. It makes me irrationally upset to have other people vying for her attention. I know it's crazy possessive. These feelings shock even me, but I've grown used to them over the weeks.

Teagan shoots me a glance from where she's sitting across from me as if she can read my thoughts. Hell, I wouldn't be surprised if she could. This woman has gotten under my skin, into my bloodstream, my bones, my thoughts, and my dreams. She owns me, body and soul. And it's about damn time she knows it.

"Let me help you with clean-up," I offer once dinner is over.

"Okay," Teagan says with a soft smile. She's still my sassy goddess, but ever since that day in the bathroom a few weeks ago, she's shown me her sweet side that was originally reserved for everyone else.

We wash and dry dishes while making small talk, but I want so much more than that. I want to tell her about my pain, my past, but I need the right opening.

Or maybe I'm just making excuses.

"Do you want to go for a ride with me tonight?" I finally ask, hoping maybe things will be easier if I get her away from the house and the other guys hanging around.

"Like in your truck?" she asks so innocently, blinking her long lashes at me. God, she has no idea how sweet and sexy she is.

I grin down at her, barely resisting the urge to kiss those soft, pink lips. "I was thinking we'd saddle up some horses. We do live on a ranch, after all. Might as well take advantage, right?"

Teagan's face flushes red, and while I love that color on her and want to see how many ways I can make her blush in bed, I never want her to be embarrassed around me. "I, um...well, I've never actually ridden a horse," she says, scrunching up her cute little nose.

"What's that, now? Never been on a horse? I think it's about time we fix that, don't you?"

Teagan gnaws on her bottom lip and finishes drying the last dish before turning to me and hitting me with those stunning blue eyes.

"It's just that. I'm kind of...well, I wouldn't say I'm *afraid* of horses..."

My eyebrows shoot up into my hairline, but I try to school my face over.

Teagan blows out a frustrated breath. "They are just so big, you know? And then have all these bulging muscles...and...they have *human* teeth." She hisses that last part out, making me laugh despite my best efforts.

"Human teeth? Baby, that's the strangest excuse I've ever heard of for someone being scared of horses."

Teagan smacks my chest and puts her hands on her hips. I barely bite back a groan at her feistiness. I want her to smack me, claw at me, bite me as I sink into her and pound her sweet pussy into the mattress until we both cum together.

"I *said* I'm not afraid of them. I just don't trust them."

"Because of their human teeth," I confirm.

She nods decisively. "And don't forget their bulging muscles. And that they are freaking giants."

I take a step closer to her and place my hands over hers where they are resting on her hips. I can't help it. She too fucking adorable and I *need* to touch some part of her to make sure she's real. Teagan doesn't move away. In fact, she leans a little closer to me, softening her stance ever so much.

"I'm a freaking giant compared to you, angel," I murmur, my eyes glued to hers. "And I have human teeth," I grin.

Teagan's breaths are becoming shallow as we both step closer together until only a few inches are separating us.

"I also have a few bulging muscles," I whisper.

She slips her hands from underneath mine so she can slide them up my arms. Her feather-light touch sends fire shooting down my spine, my heart rate spiking as lust courses through my veins.

"I've noticed," she says in the softest of whispers. We stare at each other, me holding her hips, her lightly squeezing my biceps. I want to devour her. Rip her clothes off right here and suck on her swollen nipples I see poking through her thin t-shirt. "Your teeth, I mean," Teagan clears her throat and smirks at me. "I've noticed your teeth. They are pretty nice for a dirty ranch hand."

"Dirty ranch hand? I thought I was a rodeo star?"

Teagan steps away from me, gathering the plates so she can put them away. "I have yet to see any evidence of that. For all I know, that's just what you tell all the girls who fawn all over your...teeth." She looks at me over her shoulder and winks, fucking *winks*, and I know I can't keep my distance from her for one more day.

I step up behind her, not touching her yet, just feeling the heat of her body and smelling her honey apple scent. Teagan leans back, brushing her ass against my hardening cock. I stifle a groan and rest my hands on her hips while bending down and grazing my lips up and down her neck. Her skin breaks out in goosebumps and I can feel her pulse racing against my lips as I plant a soft kiss right over it.

"Take a ride with me, love. I'm more than happy to be your first."

"M-my...first?" she says with a shaky breath.

"You're first horseback ride, of course," I say, giving her one last kiss on the side of her neck before stepping away. One more second and I would have snapped. I swear to God this tiny woman has me ready to burst in my jeans all the fucking time. I thought I had better self-control, but that was until I met Teagan.

"Oh, right. Yes. Of course," she mutters to herself. One hand reaches up and absentmindedly strokes the side of her neck where I kissed her.

"What did you think I meant?" I tease.

"Nothing. The horses. Yes. Not anything, um, not like physically. I mean...dammit," she stutters, her face going red again as she spins away from me and busies herself wiping down the counter.

Holy fuck.

I mean, I had hoped she was untouched, but I wouldn't judge her one way or another. I'm certainly no saint, though I wish I had saved myself for her. Plus, Teagan was a model in L.A. for fuck's sake. But one look at my blushing angel and I just know. She'll only ever be mine.

I gently grab her wrist and tug her towards me, wrapping her up in my arms and resting my forehead on hers.

"Love, I want to be all of your firsts. You just have to trust me, remember?"

She takes a deep breath as a slight shiver runs through her body. It's different than her tremors. This is excitement, arousal, and a little bit of fear. I can work with that. I give her hand one last squeeze and step back.

"Let's start with horses and work our way up from there, yeah?" I wink at her once she has gathered herself a bit. I love that I can make her melt. And I haven't even kissed her properly yet.

"Fine. I suppose if I can ride one huge, muscled beast, I can ride the other, right?" She grins at me and sashays her little ass towards the back door. At the last minute, she looks at me over her shoulder with a sexy eyebrow raised in challenge. "You coming, cowboy?"

"I fucking hope so," I grit out. Teagan laughs. Just like that, she has the upper hand. I don't mind.

Chapter 6

Teagan

Oh my god.

I can't believe I actually said I was going to ride Knox. I can't believe he knows I'm a virgin. I can't believe he's following me out to the stables right now. What is happening? Who am I?

My hands are shaking but it's not a bad thing this time. I'm excited. And nervous. And way out of my depth. But I'm ready for whatever Knox has in store for me. It's been three weeks of heated glances, flirty teasing, and barely-there touches.

I'm not sure what changed tonight in the kitchen while we were doing dishes, but I can't say I mind. In fact, I can still feel his lips on the side of my neck. My spine tingles and my heart pounds in my chest just remembering the heat of his body, his solid muscles pressed into my back, and if I'm not mistaken, my ass brushed up against his...

"Everything alright, angel?" Knox asks from where he's walking beside me. I swear I can feel his smooth, melted caramel voice drip down my skin. It makes me want to feel his sweat on my skin. His seed.

"Hm?" I sputter out, my face heated from the filthy images of Knox coming on my chest. I mean, what the hell? I've never had thoughts like this. Then again, I've never had inspiration quite like Knox.

He chuckles and takes my hand in his, lacing our fingers together. It's such a small thing; an innocent touch. But it has me shamefully wet all the same.

When we reach the stables, Knox strides right in and checks on some of the gigantic beasts. I follow close behind him, using Knox's large frame as a shield. Okay, so maybe I lied. I am a little scared of horses.

The more I watch Knox handle them, however, the more my anxiety fades. He's so gentle and respectful of the large creatures. I get a warm, fuzzy feeling as he checks on each one, pets them, and talks to them like they are actual humans instead of beasts with human teeth.

Knox turns around abruptly, almost knocking me right over. He wraps an arm around my back to keep me steady, pulling me into his chest and looking me over for damage.

"Sorry, love. I didn't know you were so close," he murmurs. He doesn't let go of me or break eye contact.

"I wanted to stick by you in case you needed backup," I tease, taking a step away from him. It's not that I want to, it's that I need to. If he keeps touching me, I might just melt right here on the barn floor.

Knox smirks and reaches over to grab a saddle and a few other supplies. "Backup, huh? I thought I was the dirty-ranch-hand-slash-rodeo-star. Ain't nothin' I can't handle, angel," he winks. God, I love his sparkling greenish-gray eyes, especially when he's being playful with me. I can't say anyone has ever made me smile or laugh or just joked around with me like Knox. Certainly no one in my old life.

"Pride comes before the fall, cowboy. Plus, I don't think your star status would save you if one of these animals decides to chomp down on your pretty face," I smirk.

"You think I'm pretty, huh?"

My face instantly heats. Did I say pretty? More like devastatingly gorgeous. Panty-melting. Sexy. Drool-worthy. "Not so much if you had a big bite taken out of your nose."

He laughs and shakes his head, stepping closer to me again. "You're really caught up on the teeth thing, huh?"

I shrug. "Amongst other things. A girl can't be too careful, you know." I'm trying to be fun and flirty, but there's a truth to my words I know he doesn't miss.

Knox smiles softly at me and then takes my hand. We walk over to a reddish-brown horse with a long, shiny mane and a white diamond patch on its chest. Knox sets the saddle down and rustles around in one of the saddlebags for something.

"Here," he tosses me an apple, which I somehow manage to catch. "It was left over from my lunch today. She'll like it."

"Uh, you want me to *feed* it?" I ask incredulously.

"*Her*, not it. Her name is Princess, and yes, I think feeding her is a great idea."

I stare at him, then down at the apple, then venture a look over at Princess. She is kind of beautiful. Majestic, even. But I know what she has hidden in that massive mouth of hers. Knox moves around behind me and lightly grips my hips, making me jump. I have so many things racing through my body—desire, excitement, anxiety, fear. But most of all I feel like I'm right on the edge of something big. I can't shake it. Tonight is going to change everything. I think I just might be ready for it.

"Do you trust me, Teagan?" Knox whispers, his lips tickling the shell of my ear. I nod and drag in a shaky breath. "Tell me, angel. Tell me you trust that I won't ever put you in danger. I won't ever hurt you."

"Knox..." I whisper, swallowing down the lump in my throat. He doesn't pressure me, he just waits patiently for my brain to catch up. He's steady, grounding, allowing his presence to calm me down, just like the first day I met him. I feel his lips and nose run up and down my neck, making me feel turned on, but also precious. Delicate. But I know he won't let me break. "I trust you."

He places a soft kiss right below my ear and then stands up straight. Knox takes my hand, the one not holding the apple, and raises it towards the horse. "That's it. Palm out. We're just going to pet her nose and let her get used to your scent."

I nod and let him guide my hand towards Princess. She's standing still, though I swear she's smiling at me with her big brown eyes. Knox keeps talking to me in hushed tones like I'm a frightened horse he needs to rope in. I guess I kind of am.

"Horses are very intuitive, you know. They can pick up on moods and intentions. They are also really good at reading people. I think you and Princess have a lot in common."

He stops our hands a few inches away from her face and lets her come to us the rest of the way. I gasp quietly when the coarse hair glides against my palm. It's rougher than I thought it would be, but Princess is warm and surprisingly gentle. Knox keeps on talking to me as we pet the beautiful beast.

"She's a rescue horse. Isaiah told me that she was wandering around outside of the property a few years ago, all skin and bones."

"Like me," I whisper, half teasing.

"You're beautiful, love. All of you. Always have been. I'm just glad you and Princess are happy and healthy." I nod, letting his words fill me up. Happy and healthy. Two words I never thought would describe me. "Princess here was skittish at first, understandably so. Isaiah worked with her and earned her trust. Now she's one of the calmest, most gentle horses I've ever met."

Knox takes my other hand in his, holding the apple out for Princess to eat. My hand trembles, but he holds me steady. Princess sniffs at the offering and then opens her slobbery lips, revealing those huge, freakish teeth. I instinctively jerk my hand back, but Knox grips my hand firmly, not letting me run away scared.

I watch in equal parts terror and fascination as she opens her mouth and gingerly takes a huge bite, careful to avoid our hands. She snorts appreciatively and goes back for the second half of the apple, licking the palm of my hand and making me giggle. Princess sniffs up my arm and nuzzles into my hand once again.

"See? Not so ferocious, huh?"

"Yeah. Not so bad," I agree. Princess gives me a sassy look and lifts her head up as if to show me she's pretty damn great. I laugh and pet the side of her face, no longer afraid of her. Knox steps away from me and saddles her up, leaving me there to get better acquainted with my new friend.

After a few minutes, I look over at Knox, who is just standing beside Princess and looking at me with something unrecognizable in his eyes.

"What?" I ask self-consciously.

"Nothin," he smiles. "You're just so damn beautiful."

I roll my eyes and blush at his words. I've been called beautiful before, praised for my small figure, high cheekbones, and long legs. But it always felt empty to me. Not Knox, however. I know he's looking beyond the skin-deep beauty and peering straight into my soul when he says those words.

"You're not too bad yourself," I wink.

"Right. With my pretty face and all."

I sigh at the same time Princess does, making Knox laugh. "I knew you two would get along. Maybe a little too well," he chuckles. He leads Princess out of the stable and out into the open. "Are you ready, angel?"

"What about your horse?"

"I thought we'd ride together this time. I can give you a proper riding lesson later."

The thought of being so close to Knox has a delicious shiver running down my spine, settling in my throbbing pussy and making me ache in a way I never have before.

"Sounds good," I squeak out.

Knox grins and reaches out for my hand, tugging me towards the saddle and directing me where to put my hands and legs. He hoists me up, his grip firm and commanding on my hips as I swing my leg over and straddle the large creature. I'm barely settled in before Knox pulls himself up and squeezes in behind me, pulling my back to his front and looping an arm around my waist.

We start off trotting slowly, and I must admit, it's kind of thrilling being so high up, letting Princess take us wherever Knox is leading.

I feel Knox squeeze his thighs slightly against the sides of the horse, making my heart beat faster. Princess goes a little faster at his urging, and I gasp, clinging to Knox's strong arm he has wrapped around me.

"I've got you," he says, kissing the top of my head.

I breathe in deep and enjoy the ride, relaxing into Knox's hard muscles and letting him have control. I've never felt safer, more protected, more cared for in my entire life.

Before long, we're slowing down and then stopping next to a little stream. Knox dismounts and then helps me down, tying Princess to a nearby tree.

"It's gorgeous out here. I can't believe this is the first time I've seen the rest of the property," I say, walking over to the edge of the stream and looking out over the rolling hills bathed in the waning light of the evening.

"I didn't realize how much I missed working on ranches like this until I came back," Knox says quietly, standing behind me and wrapping his arms around my waist, pulling me against him. He rests his chin on top of my head and I can't help but think that we fit perfectly.

"Why did you leave in the first place? Why the rodeo?"

He sighs and buries his face into my hair, breathing me in. It makes me smile, thinking maybe I ground him as much as he grounds me.

"There are the obvious answers, like the adrenaline rush after a ride, thrill-seeking, never being one to back down from a challenge. But truthfully, it was my uncle who pushed me into it. I never knew my dad, it was just my mom and me growing up, and my uncle Anthony. He lived next door to us, helped out whenever he could. He did the junior circuit when he was a kid and then worked his way up to the amateur league. I loved going to the rodeo and watching him and the other cowboys. Anthony always took me around to the different events and introduced me to everyone. I felt like one of the guys, you know?

Believe it or not, I was a scrawny kid and I got picked on a lot at school, so having friends and family like that..."

Knox sighs and squeezes me tightly. My heart hurts at the thought of anyone being mean to my Knox. How dare they? I want to poke their eyes out with some nasty six-inch stilettos. He takes a deep breath before continuing.

"Anthony taught me everything he knew. He entered me in my first rodeo. And second. And fiftieth. He was so proud of me when I rose up through the ranks. Uncle Anthony came to every single one of my events, even when..." Knox clears the obvious emotion from his throat. "Even when he was diagnosed with liver cancer."

Tears prick my eyes for the loss and heartache he's had to endure. I spin around in his arms and hug Knox so tightly my arms go numb. He hugs me right back, tucking my head under his chin and rocking me back and forth as if I'm the one who needs comfort. "I'm so sorry," I mumble into his chest.

"I worked part-time on a ranch with Noah for my senior year of high school and then full time for a few years after to help pay for treatments. I kept up my career and joined the Professional Bull Riders when things took a turn for the worse. My first ride with PBR was against a bull named Thrasher. It was the last bull my uncle rode before he got his diagnosis and had to end his career. I was determined to beat the fucking bull, but I was thrown after two seconds."

I gasp and cling to him even tighter. The idea of anything happening to my Knox sends me into a tailspin. Somehow, in such a short amount of time, I realize this beautiful, strong, kind cowboy has become everything to me. I think I might even lo—

No. I can't go there.

"I felt like such a failure, but Anthony consoled me, just like he always did. In the last conversation we had before he passed, Anthony said he wanted me to get back on the bull, to have an undefeated career, and then kick Thrasher in the balls the next opportunity I got. Well,

Thrasher is retired, but his bloodline lives on in a new bull, Tank. That's why this last ride is so important to me. It's not just my record on the line, it's Anthony's memory."

I nod, trying to understand. I do, in a way. But I also selfishly want that part of Knox's life to be over. It feels like we were different people before we met and now we're ready to start a new life together. Or at least I am. I know it's selfish of me to want him to give that up, and really, it's moving way too fast. A life together? Marriage? Kids? I want all of that so bad it hurts.

I don't know what comes over me. Maybe it's the weight of his confession, or my own confusing feelings, or the need to comfort him. Either way, I tilt my head up and press my lips to his. Knox doesn't hesitate. He moves his lips with mine, taking over the kiss and prying my lips open with his tongue.

I moan softly and let him in, gasping at the need behind each stroke of his tongue. I taste his longing, his promises, his desire for me. For us. Gripping his hips, I pull him closer to me, desperate for more of him. Knox groans and tangles his hands in my hair, angling me right where he wants me so he can delve deeper into my mouth. He's all-consuming, his citrus and leather scent, the warmth of his mouth, his hard length rubbing against my stomach.

"God, Teagan, I've wanted this for so long," he murmurs into my lips before taking them again, claiming them as his own. I roll my hips against him and slide my hands up his chest, fisting the collar of his shirt and clinging to him with everything I am.

Knox tears his mouth away from mine, only to nip and kiss down my neck. I whimper when I feel his hands slide down my back so slowly, taking his time to feel every inch of me before gripping my ass in his large, capable hands.

We're lost in each other, completely taken over by the lust and longing that has been building up between us for weeks. Eventually, Knox pries himself away from me, giving me one last chaste kiss on the lips before resting his forehead on mine. We're both panting, sharing the same air, and basking in the intimacy we've both craved for so long.

"Best first kiss ever," I whisper, smiling nervously. I don't know why I said that except that he makes me feel comfortable to say pretty much anything. I felt that even the very first day I met him and started mouthing off. I've never been sassy or bratty, but I felt like I had to push the boundaries with Knox, knowing the whole time he'd still chase after me relentlessly.

Some deep, gravelly noise bubbles up from Knox's chest as he tips his head back and takes a deep breath.

"Fuck, angel. You have no idea what that does to me," he groans almost painfully.

"What?" I ask, genuinely confused.

"Knowing I'm the only one to touch you like this. To see you all disheveled, your lips bruised, your eyes glossed over. It'll only ever be me, love. You understand that, right? There's no going back now. You're mine."

I chew on my bottom lip nervously, wanting his words to be true but having a hard time believing this isn't all a dream.

Knox takes my silence for uncertainty and cups my face so sweetly. "We'll go as slow as you want. I'll never take anything you don't willingly give me."

"I know," I whisper, tilting my head up so our lips are inches apart. "I trust you. With all of me." With that, I kiss him again, letting him know I want this, I want him more than words can say. Each swipe of his tongue and nip of his teeth open up a need deep inside of me. There's a tugging low in my belly, an almost painful throbbing.

After years of working in an industry that treats sex and sensuality as something to be marketed, I thought I had become desensitized to all of it. But not with Knox. He's awoken some dark, primal need inside of me, one that I know only he can fulfill.

"Gotta stop, baby," he grunts into the side of my neck before licking me there and catching the tender skin between his teeth. "I can't hold back much longer, and I don't want to scare you away."

"I'm not scared," I breathe out. "I can't hold back either. I just...I don't know what I'm doing. Can you show me?"

"Fuck," he growls, attacking my lips and lifting me up in his arms, making me gasp. I automatically wrap my legs around him and hang on tight as he carries me towards a large oak tree. Gently setting me down, Knox grips my hips and walks me backward until my back is up against the tree. "Are you wet for me, Teagan? Is my dirty little angel wet for me?"

I let out a throaty moan and nod. "Will you... Can you... T-touch me there?"

"Fuck yes," he grits out, cupping my pussy and rubbing my aching center over my jeans. "Goddamn, I feel your heat. Do you need something from me? Does this pretty little kitty need to cum?"

His words are so filthy, but they trigger something inside of me. This man has reduced me to base urges I didn't think I had until I met him. I nod and roll my hips, trying to get him to somehow touch me deeper, more, more, more...

Knox nips at my chin, my pulse point, my shoulder, and then slips his hand into my jeans. I know he feels how soaked I am, and it only turns him on more.

"Jesus," he grunts, stroking my pussy and parting my folds over my panties. The fabric scrapes against my sensitive clit, making me shiver and moan.

"More," I beg, gripping his meaty biceps and digging my nails in.

Knox plays with the waistband of my panties, teasing me and driving me absolutely wild. Finally, *finally*, he touches me where I'm throbbing for him, swiping two fingers up my slit and circling my clit.

"Teagan, shit, angel, this cunt is so fucking juicy," he grunts. My pussy contracts at his dirty words, trying to suck him inside. He groans and continues to stroke me up and down, gathering my arousal and massaging my little ball of nerves.

I squeeze my eyes shut and moan, throwing my head back and exposing my neck to his greedy mouth. Knox sucks on the side of my neck and dips one finger into my tight hole, making me grind down on his hand. "Oh," I gasp, pulsing around him and releasing even more wetness.

"So fucking tight. You're gonna feel fucking incredible wrapped around my dick, aren't you, love? Do you want me to stretch out this little cunt of yours?"

"Mmm..." I nod frantically, shifting my hips and forcing his finger deeper inside of me. "Fuck!" I cry out.

Suddenly, Knox removes his hand, leaving me empty and confused. I open my eyes and see Knox kneeling in front of me, gliding his hands up and down my thighs. "I need to taste you. Just one taste. Is that okay? Can I make you cum on my tongue?"

"God yes," I whimper. I don't even care that I'm begging him. Knox created this mess, now he needs to lick it up. Who am I right now? Whose filthy thoughts are these? I don't have time to think about that for long. Knox practically rips my jeans open, tugging them down my legs along with my soaking panties.

"Jesus, how do you smell so good?" he says more to himself than to me.

Knox slips my shoes off and helps me step out of my jeans, staring at my pussy the whole time. I should probably be embarrassed or have at least a few reservations, right? I mean, we're out in the open, I just had my first kiss, and now I'm going to let him eat me out?

Hell yes, I am.

I tremble as he ghosts his fingers up my legs, guiding one over his shoulder, exposing me completely to him.

"Perfect, just like the rest of you," he whispers right before parting my lips with his tongue and sucking on my clit. Hard.

I buck my hips and grab his hair, overwhelmed by the sensation of his warm tongue against my sensitive, swollen clit. He growls into my pussy, the vibrations rattling my bones as he devours me.

Knox spears his tongue into my entrance and swirls his nose around my clit. My breaths come out as short little gasps as my muscles tense and pulse. It's unlike anything I've ever experienced. I feel myself teetering on the edge, close, so close to falling over into the unknown.

I open my mouth to tell him I've never cum before, but a strangled scream comes out instead as I explode on his tongue. I jerk in his arms, but Knox grips me tighter, steadying my movements even as he laps at me and bats my clit around, prolonging my pleasure.

He looks up at me right as I tip my head down to look at him. His eyes are stormy, dark, and feral. I see my juices covering his lips and nose, making me moan. Knox doesn't give me any time to recover before flattening his tongue and licking me from bottom to top.

"Oh, ohmygod, Knox, I... I can't..."

He grunts and continues to nibble and suck on my folds. The world crashes down around me until all I can focus on are the relentless strokes of his tongue as he pushes me higher and higher, winds me tighter and tighter, increasing the pressure in my core almost unbearably.

I gasp and writhe as he plunges two fingers inside of me and curls them up, hitting some spot inside me that makes my nerves light up and burn deliciously beneath my skin. He swirls his tongue around my clit again and again. I can't breathe. My heart thrashes. There's a rushing sensation flooding my body. I feel like I have to twist away, back down from the onslaught of pleasure, but I can't. I'm rooted in place, completely at his mercy.

My whole body gets tight. The pressure builds inside me, through my pelvis, over my skin, in my muscles, and along nerves. Pleasure swells and explodes as I convulse in his arms. He pins me to the tree, mercilessly eating me out with a growl. My sweaty flesh shakes as I jerk and fight my way through my orgasm.

"Oh baby," he raises his face to stare at me in awe. "You squirted all over me. Shit, you're incredible. Love making this perfect little pussy gush."

I'm floating through space, through bliss, through lust and release. There's a rhythmic, sharp throbbing between my legs that brings me down from my high. I open my eyes and see Knox slowly licking me up and down, swallowing down all of me, every last drop.

My bones turn to liquid as I slump against the tree completely wrung out. Knox helps me get my jeans and shoes on and then stands up, pulling me into his chest. He holds me up and kisses me, letting me taste myself. He groans and I bury my face in his chest, not sure what happens next.

"Are you okay, love? You're shaking," he whispers. "Was that too much?"

I shake my head and kiss his chest before lifting my head up to look him in his beautiful gray eyes. "You're my first in every single way." I hope he knows what I mean without me having to say it.

His brow furrows, but then his eyes grow wide as understanding sinks in. "Was that your first orgasm, love?"

I nod, my cheeks heating up.

"Teagan, God," he murmurs, kissing my forehead. "You're amazing. My dirty, sweet angel. I swear you're not even real."

I laugh softly at his admission. "I can't believe you're real either," I whisper.

He holds me for long moments, proving to both of us that this is real. We're real. And we somehow found each other.

Chapter 7

Knox

"Did you talk to your girl?" Noah asks me the next morning after breakfast. We're loading up one of the work trucks and getting ready to do some major yard work on the north end of the ranch.

I shoot him an annoyed look, but I can't hide my smirk. "You just need to hear that you were right."

"Nah, I don't need to hear it to know it's true," he chuckles. "You're welcome, by the way. I want to be a groomsman at the wedding," he winks.

"What wedding?" Jacob buts in, helping us load up the truck.

"My wedding," I say with a smile. "But only if I get the family discount on the wedding venue." I give Noah a pointed look.

Noah laughs while Jacob gawks at me. "How serious are you right now? I know your plan is to marry the woman, but have you asked her? Are you dating? Does she think it's just a fling?"

"Why, Noah, I never took you for gossiping type," Jacob smirks. He's the light-hearted goofball of the bunch. Noah thumps him on the back of the head and Jacob shoves him away, laughing the whole time.

"Smartass," Noah mutters under his breath before turning his attention back to me. "I'm just saying. Jade told me a little bit about Teagan's life back in L.A., bein' a model and all that messed up shit with her mom. The woman has been used for her beauty for her whole life, I just want to make sure you didn't take her out to the barn to have your way with her and then drop her off at her cabin like nothing happened."

"What are you insinuating, Noah?" I snap, all playfulness dropping from my demeanor.

"Calm down," he says, with his hands out. "I know you're not like that, at least not with her. I get that you're in it for the long haul. But does Teagan know that? Have you had a real conversation with her about the future?"

"Of course," I say defensively, although now I'm not sure if I've actually put into words how I've felt about her from the moment I laid eyes on her. "I mean, I told her she's mine. And we've..."

"Done the deed?" Noah supplies.

"What are you, seventy-five?" Jacob laughs at him. I should probably shoo him away, but I feel comfortable around all of these guys. They'll all know Teagan is mine soon enough.

"All I'm sayin' is that you both disappeared real quick after dinner and Jade saw you walking Teagan to her cabin after sunset. You're both consenting adults and I don't want the details." Noah shivers and grimaces, though all I can do is smirk arrogantly remembering the way I made my angel cum three times and squirt in my fucking mouth. Goddamn. She's perfection. "Knox!" Noah barks, breaking me out of my filthy thoughts.

"What?" I grunt. "First you want me to be careful, and now you're telling me to propose?"

"I'm saying you need to DTR."

Jacob bursts out laughing until Noah glares at him. Jacob takes the hint and saunters off to take care of something else.

"DTR?" I ask.

"Define the relationship. Who's the old man now?"

"Still you," I shoot back. "If you know any slang it's from Jade. You're not fooling me." I shake my head and throw a roll of trash bags at Noah.

"The point still stands. You can't just growl out *mine* and expect Teagan to know what that entails. Or at least that what Jade tells me. It's called being an alpha-hole."

I have to stop and catch my breath, I'm laughing so hard. God, Noah is trying so hard to give me relationship advice via Jade. I can just picture the two of them gossiping about us and Jade urging him to give me some big talk. I'm not even mad about it. In fact, it makes me happy that they care about Teagan and me enough to meddle. Inspiration strikes me and I know I have Noah in a position where he can't say no.

"Give Teagan the night off. I want to cook for her in my cabin and *DTR*," I say, wagging my eyebrows just to see Noah squirm. He doesn't disappoint.

"If you promise never to talk about the things you do behind closed doors—"

"Or in open fields, barns, back seats of cars..."

"Fucking hell, any of that, if you promise to never breathe a word of that to me, I'll let Jade know we're responsible for dinner tonight."

"I appreciate your permission, *boss*. I also think if I asked Jade myself, she'd be over the moon excited and give Teagan and me the rest of the day off."

"She's a softie, that one. Good thing she has me to crack a few heads when need be," Noah grumbles.

I consider making fun of him a little more but decide against it. I already have what I want, which is an entire evening alone with my angel.

***

Despite Noah giving me a hard time, he let me cut out early for the day so I could wash up and figure out dinner plans. I thought about taking Teagan out but ultimately decided to cook for her. I know she's still anxious around crowds and new people, and while I want to help her overcome all of those fears, I want her to be comfortable tonight. I'm not expecting anything more from her physically, but God, a guy can hope.

I was so fucking hard after eating out her sweet little pussy last night. Jesus, licking her soft, tender skin, drinking down her sweet sticky mess as she came again and again. fuck me. My woman is a goddess and she has no idea.

It took every ounce of willpower not to rip my jeans open and jack off while my face was buried in between her creamy thighs, but I knew it would be too much for her. She had her first kiss, her first orgasm, and even though it physically pained me to keep my cock stuffed into my jeans, I didn't want to overwhelm her or make her feel pressured to do anything else. I had to walk over to the stream and splash my face with cold water just to get the monster in my pants to relax enough to ride back to the stables.

Noah is right though. My angel is so much more than the star of my dirty, dirty dreams. She's everything. My future. My wife. The mother of my children. She's precious, loved, protected, and safe in my arms. That's what I mean when I say she's mine. And that's exactly what I plan on showing her tonight.

I stroll into the kitchen a little after four, hoping to catch Teagan before she starts getting dinner ready. When I don't see her right away, I head into the living room and stop short when I see her curled up in the large bay window sipping on some sweet tea. Her white-blonde hair is piled on top of her head, revealing her slender neck to me. She's looking out of the window with her long legs tucked up underneath her.

"Hey love," I say softly, not wanting to startle her. Teagan turns her head towards me and rewards me with the brightest smile I've ever seen. I swear my heart stutters in my chest and then beats in double time to catch up. Her eyes rake up and down my body, and hell yeah, my dick takes notice.

"Hi," she whispers, a slight blush creeping into her pale cheeks.

"Thinking dirty thoughts, are we?" I tease, closing the distance between us and standing in front of her.

"Maybe a little," she admits, uncurling herself from the window and turning towards me with her legs slightly parted. I step in between her legs, barely suppressing a groan at the idea of Teagan having the same filthy fantasies as me.

"Me too, angel. All fucking day. It's a bitch trying to bale hay while fighting off an erection the size of Texas." I worry I went too far, but then her eyes drift down to my lengthening cock and she licks her lips. Jesus, this woman is going to kill me.

"Can I help with that?" The words are tentative but so goddamn sweet coming from her lips. I can tell she means it but is still shy. I plan to strip her of her insecurities, amongst other things.

"You have no idea how much I want that. But first, let me take you to dinner."

"Really?"

The surprised tone behind her words twists my gut. Noah really was right. I didn't make my intentions clear last night. That shit ends here.

"Of course." I tuck a few strands of loose hair behind her ear and cup her chin. "I went a little crazy last night and I think I might have given you the wrong impression."

"What impression is that?" she whispers, biting her bottom lip and looking up at me so innocently and yet so seductively. How the hell she pulls that off is beyond me, but damn if it doesn't make me want to throw her over my shoulder and carry her off to my cabin. Fuck, that's the opposite of what I'm trying to show her.

"I want it all with you. Not just your body, but your heart. Your past, your pain, your future. I know that's scary, and I know you don't give your trust out to just anyone, but—"

"I trust you," she says easily. "I never thought you were in it just for...*sex,*" she whispers the last word, making me smile. It's going to be so wonderful to corrupt my angel. "I mean, I'm totally inexperienced and I haven't even really done anything to you yet, I just took and took and didn't give anything back. Plus, I was the one who kissed you first, remember? If anything, I'm using you."

I chuckle at her response, bending down and kissing her temple and then nibbling on her earlobe. "You can use me anytime, love. I always want you to take your pleasure first. I promise it's just as enjoyable for me as it is for you."

She laughs at that, the sweet sound lingering in my ears. "I don't know about that. I definitely got the better end of the deal last night."

I can't help but steal a kiss from her. It's far too short, but it's absolutely necessary for my own sanity.

"I'll pick you up in an hour," I say once I tear myself away from her.

"Huh?" Teagan says all breathily. "Tonight? What? I have to cook dinner! Where are we going? I don't have anything fancy to wear and I...I..."

"Shh, baby, it's okay," I murmur, kissing the crease between her eyebrows. "You have the night off. I'm cooking you dinner at my place. No crowds. No need to dress up. You're perfect just the way you are."

She tilts her head to the side, considering my words for a moment before rewarding me with another one of her brilliant smiles. "Okay."

That one word has never been more beautiful.

"Now shoo so I can get ready. You may not care what I look like, but I'm not wearing yoga pants and a messy bun for my first real date."

"Huh. I guess this is my first real date too," I muse.

"Really? I get to be one of your firsts?"

I nod and wink at her. She has no idea that she's more than just my first date. She's the first woman I've ever loved. The first person who made me feel like I belong. The first person who has made me want to fight for more, to give her the whole world. All in good time.

An hour later, I'm knocking on the door of Teagan's little cabin. I have dinner all planned out and it shouldn't take too long to throw it all together. The cabins don't have a very large kitchen, seeing as most meals are served in the main house, but there's a small stovetop, a mini-fridge, and a microwave.

I hear Teagan inside her cabin, walking towards the door. She's just on the other side, I can sense it. Teagan takes a big breath and blows it out, almost as if she's nervous. Silly girl. There's nothing she could do to mess this up. I'm all fucking in with her, no matter what.

When she opens the door, I have to take a step back to fully admire her beauty. She's in skin-tight jeans and a blue blouse that matches her stunning blue eyes. Her silky blonde hair cascades over her shoulders in loose waves, begging me to run my fingers through it. Teagan has some light makeup on, but nothing over the top. She doesn't need it at all, but I love that she went through the effort to dress up for me. The outfit is complete with cowgirl boots that only reach to the top of her ankle, giving her a classy country girl look. I love it.

"You're absolutely gorgeous, love. Are you ready to go?"

She nods and takes my hand, lacing our fingers together. We barely make it inside of my cabin before Teagan turns and presses her soft curves into me, kissing me lightly on the mouth. I grip her hips and back her into the wall, deepening our kiss and combing my fingers through her hair.

"Sorry," she pants once we break for air. "You just...you make me crazy whenever you're around."

"You make me crazy too," I mumble into the side of her neck before kissing her there.

Reluctantly, I step away from her and lead her over to the couch. This is the only cabin with a gorgeous fireplace. I've never used it before tonight, but I built a big fire in hopes we could curl up by it later. Or sooner. I wouldn't complain either way.

Once I get Teagan some sweet tea and get dinner started, I join her on the couch while the food cooks. I take her boots off and place her feet in my lap so I can give her a massage. Teagan giggles and kicks her cute little feet out as soon as I touch them.

"Are you ticklish?" I laugh in surprise.

"Maybe a little," she admits, trying to escape from my grasp.

I grin devilishly at her and begin rubbing my hands up her legs, loving the way she squirms and laughs.

"That is just *so* good to know, angel," I say, finally relenting. She tries to pull away from me, but I grab her legs and place them back on my lap. Teagan sighs dramatically, but I catch the small smile tugging at her lips.

We talk about her time at the ranch so far, how she got into cooking, and what her goals are. Not surprisingly, she doesn't have much of a game plan beyond working here. This was her escape, her place to regroup. I'm more than happy to provide whatever future she sees for herself.

She helps me set the table once the timer goes off for our dinner. It's so easy being around her, so natural to be preparing dinner together and sitting down to share a meal. Yeah, we've done it dozens of times over the last few weeks, but this is different. It's just me and her. Oh, and our ridiculous lust and longing. All throughout the meal she's giving me heated glances and knocking her knee against mine or finding little ways to touch me. I'm shamelessly flirting, trying to see all of the ways I can make her blush.

When dinner is over, Teagan gets up and starts to clear off the table. I stand up and tug her into my chest instead, kissing her thoroughly before spinning her out of my arms and pulling her back into me, dipping her low.

She laughs and loops her arms around my neck, holding on tightly. She doesn't let go when I pull her back up and start dancing with her, humming an old tune softly in her ear as we sway back and forth.

"You're a dirty cowboy, rodeo star, excellent chef, amazing kisser, and now a dancer, too?" Teagan teases, looking up at me with those glittering blue eyes of hers.

"Mmhmm, I'm just full of surprises," I wink at her, dipping her down low again, taking the opportunity to nip her neck and kiss away the sting.

"Where did you learn to dance? I can't picture you taking lessons."

"My momma taught me. She said a man who can cook and dance will always get the girl. I just never wanted to keep anyone until you," I tell her truthfully. Teagan grins up at me, letting me know my words were the exact right thing to say.

"Your momma sounds like a smart lady."

"Indeed. She'll love you. She always wanted a daughter, but she got three rowdy boys instead."

"I'm gonna meet her?"

"Of course. I'll take you to her house for Sunday dinner when I get back from my last ride. She has a big celebration planned, though she thinks it's a surprise."

A flash of worry crosses Teagan's face, and I know what's going through her mind. She doesn't like thinking about me riding Thrasher. I brush a soft kiss onto her lips, hoping to distract her. It works surprisingly well.

She digs her nails into the back of my neck, pulling me closer and taking my lips in a searing kiss. I grip her hips and mold our bodies together, losing my self-control with each desperate swipe of her tongue. Backing her into the kitchen, I lift her easily onto the counter and step in between her legs. Teagan moans and grinds her pussy against the growing bulge in my pants.

"Fuck, I feel your heat. You need something from me, angel?"

She nods and licks her lips, biting down on her bottom lip and looking up at me with a heated desire that matches my own. "I need everything from you," she whispers.

I groan and close my eyes, resting my forehead on hers. My dick is pressing against my zipper painfully just thinking about giving her everything. Every. Fucking. Inch.

"Are you sure? I swear this night isn't about that, but fuck, angel, I want everything with you too."

"I'm sure. I'm ready. I can't explain it, I just... I need you."

"You have me, angel."

"Then show me what's mine."

I growl and lift her up in my arms, carrying her to the king-sized bed in the corner of the one-room cabin. I set her down on her feet and begin unbuttoning her blouse, kissing every inch of newly exposed skin. My lips never leave her luscious body as I peel her shirt off and then work the button of her jeans. I slide them off, along with her panties, kissing up her smooth legs as I stand back up.

My angel is standing before me in just a black lacy bra. I lean down and tug at one of the cups with my teeth, pulling it down so I can suck on her pebbled nipple.

"Oh!" She gasps in surprise, making me growl into her soft flesh and bite down just enough to leave a little mark. Fuck, I can barely rip my mouth away from her skin to remove her bra.

When she's completely naked, I step back and feast on her gorgeous body. I can't believe this beautiful creature is offering herself to me, giving me her body, her virginity, and hopefully, her heart.

I gently lay her down on the bed, taking time to admire the soft glow of the fire against her pale skin.

"God, you're stunning, Teagan. So fucking beautiful, love."

I tuck her hair behind her ear and trail my fingers across her jaw, down her throat, between her breasts, and down her torso, circling them around her belly button. Teagan giggles, her little tummy shaking with laughter as she squirms away from me.

"Another ticklish spot?" I grin, quirking an eyebrow up.

"Maybe..." She smiles at me. Fuck, she's so beautiful. I love seeing her like this, naked, spread out, eyes gleaming with laughter and lust. She's every single one of my dreams come true. "I want to see you too, ya know. I might not be experienced, but I think both of us have to be naked for this to work."

I growl and tear at my clothes, suddenly needing her skin on my skin, her taste in my mouth, her pussy wrapped around my cock. I take a deep breath, trying to rein it in a bit. This is her first time. I can't fuck her like an animal. Yet.

Crawling over her supple body, I kiss her breasts, the hollow of her throat, her jaw, and finally her lips. She wraps her legs around me and rocks her hips up and down.

"Slow down, baby. I need to make sure you're ready for me," I murmur. My words say one thing, but my body doesn't get the message. I roll my hips in time with her, settling my aching cock along her slit and tapping her clit with each thrust.

"I'm ready," she moans, tipping her head back.

I manage to grip her thighs and pry her legs off of me so I can slide down her body and position myself in front of her dripping pussy.

"Fuck, you are ready. So goddamn wet for me."

Teagan nods her head frantically, thrusting her hips up involuntarily. I lick her from bottom to top, sucking on her swollen ball of nerves. She's already shaking and panting for me and I can tell she's right on the edge. I reach up with one hand and pinch her nipple while biting down softly on her clit.

She erupts for me, giving me all of her release as I greedily lick up every drop. Teagan grips my hair and pulls me up, the dark look in her eyes letting me know she needs more. I crawl back up her body, placing sloppy, open-mouthed kisses on her hips, her tummy, her breasts. She's writhing underneath me and then moans as I kiss her deeply.

"Gonna pop your cherry with your taste in my mouth, angel. Is that what you want?"

"God yes, stop teasing me, I need you," she whimpers.

I suck on her neck and reach down in between us, plunging two fingers into her tight little hole, stretching her out for me. I find her g-spot easily, groaning when she pulses around me and cries out. I stroke the rough patch of skin over and over until her legs are shaking and she can barely breathe. Right before she cums, I withdraw my fingers and sink my ten inches inside of her in one long thrust.

"Oh fuck!" she yells, coming instantly. I hold myself still, feeling her orgasm pulse and throb around my cock. She clings to me and whimpers, dragging in shallow breaths until her muscles finally relax.

I look down at her flushed face, a few tears gathering in her eyes and falling. I kiss them away and rest my forehead on hers.

"Are you okay, love?"

"Yeah...I...I didn't know what to expect but you..." She sighs and opens her eyes, staring straight down into my soul. "You feel good. I'm so full... It's overwhelming but perfect."

"You're perfect, Teagan. So damn perfect. Can I move?" I grit out, trying like hell to hold onto some semblance of sanity, but she's making it damn near impossible to think about anything else other than pounding her into the mattress and filling her up with my cum.

Instead of answering with words, Teagan shifts her hips, lodging me deeper inside of her. I growl savagely and bite my lip to keep from fucking her into the mattress.

"Shit," she breathes out, jerking her hips again to get me deeper.

That's it.

I fucking break.

I pull back and then plunge in deeper. She moans, her eyes fluttering shut as I rock into her, grinding my cock into her sweet pussy and feeling every inch of her ripe, wet heaven. Once I feel her inner walls pulse and beg for more, my control slips completely.

My hips slam against hers and I groan when I see her perfect, round tits bouncing in time with my thrusts. I pick up speed, holding her in place as I take what she saved just for me. The wet slap of our bodies fills the room, along with the beautiful sound of my name on her lips. She rakes her nails down my arms as she drops her head back, completely surrendered to her pleasure.

"So tight and perfect for me, love. You feel so good, fuck, better than anything I could have ever imagined."

Teagan moans and crosses her ankles behind my back as she bites my bottom lip and kisses me with ferocious hunger. I grunt and snap my hips against hers, feeling every sweet, sticky inch of her drenched pussy.

"Yes, oh yes, right there," she cries out, arching her back and pressing her tits into my chest.

I dip my head down and rest my cheek against hers as I hammer that spot over and over, loving the sound of her breathy moans in my ear.

"I'm... I'm..."

"I know, love, I feel you. Cum for me, angel. Cum all over my fucking cock."

Her entire body arches and tenses, expanding before she curls in on herself and screams into my neck, biting down as her orgasm devastates her tiny body. I grit my teeth as cum rises up my shaft, watching as her head tips back and moan after moan pours from her swollen lips. I rut into her, feeling her release another wave of wetness all over my shaft.

I lock my arms and look down at where we are connected. I feel the way we are no longer separate people, but one. That thought tips me over the edge, sending me crashing into an intense orgasm that steals my breath and strength.

I shake and pump into her again and again, shooting rope after rope of cum deep inside that convulsing cunt, praying it takes hold and gets her pregnant this first time. I feel a little selfish not even talking to her about protection, but we both know this is forever. I'll always take care of her and all of our children. I'm hoping for at least three.

My arms give out and I collapse on top of her. I roll over and drag her with me, never breaking our connection as I settle her on my chest with her straddling me. Teagan whimpers with each exhale, her pussy still quivering around me with little aftershocks.

I tuck her into my chest and stroke her back in a calming gesture, bringing her down gently. We stay like that for long moments, our hearts beating rapidly and then slowing down together. Teagan is completely limp in my arms, making me smile.

"You okay, love?" I murmur, not wanting to break this little bubble we're in, but needing to make sure I didn't hurt her.

"So good," she slurs, snuggling deeper into my chest.

I grin and kiss the top of her head, reaching over to grab the blankets and cover us up.

"Me too, angel. Me too."

She sighs contentedly and kisses my chest. If I wasn't already a goner for her, that would have sealed the deal. So fucking sweet and sexy.

"I've got you, love. Get some rest now."

Teagan mumbles something that sounds like I love you, but before I get a chance to ask her about it, I hear her softly snoring.

"I love you too, angel," I whisper.

Chapter 8

Teagan

The first thing I notice when I wake up is that I'm wrapped around a furnace. No, not a furnace. A man. A big, hard, muscled man who is also naked and snoring softly. The second thing I notice is the incessant ringing of the alarm on my phone, letting me know it's way too damn early and I have to get ready for the day.

I try to untangle myself from Knox, but he's got an arm wrapped around the small of my back, holding me close to his chest, and his leg is draped over my thigh, essentially locking me in place. I giggle at how possessive my cowboy is, even in his sleep.

"Mmph, uuuhg," he mumbles, burying his face into the side of my neck. I laugh again, more loudly this time. Who knew Knox was so grumpy and adorable in the morning?

"I have to get up," I tell him, kissing him on his forehead.

"No. Mine," he says, still half asleep. Knox tightens his hold on me, tucking my head under his chin, essentially suffocating me. I don't mind.

But my alarm does. It goes off again, making Knox groan and wake up a little more.

"Let me at least turn my alarm off," I reason with him.

"Noooo..." he whines. I squirm in his arms, fighting my way out of his embrace. Knox shifts slightly and sighs, loosening his hold on me so I can reach over and grab my phone. The instant my alarm is silenced, Knox loops his arms around me and pulls me back into his chest.

"Knox," I giggle. "I have to get up and go make breakfast."

"Uh-uh," he says like a stubborn toddler.

"Uh-huh," I say right back. "I already skipped out on dinner, thanks to you. The guys will be worthless on the ranch without some sustenance."

"Fuck them," he mumbles, rolling on top of me and kissing down my neck. "Actually, fuck me," he murmurs before sucking on my nipple and making me groan.

"Knox..." I plead, though I'm not sure if I'm pleading for him to continue or to let me go. Okay, that's not true. I'm begging him to continue.

I shift underneath him and spread my legs, allowing him to settle his hips in between my thighs.

"Need you, angel. Need you so fucking bad," he groans, kissing me deeply and grinding his hard cock against my pussy. "Jesus, you need me too, don't you? You're so wet for me."

I rock my hips up and down his shaft, growing wetter by the second. He's right. I need him desperately. Knox pulls back slightly, lining his hard shaft up with my entrance.

"Are you sore, love?" he asks, poised right at my opening, his forehead resting on mine.

"Only in the best way."

Knox groans and pushes his way inside of me, slowly, so slowly. I gasp, getting used to his size again. I still can't believe he fits inside of me. The man has a huge dick. And that's an understatement.

"Fuck, you feel so good, so tight," he mumbles, still groggy and impossibly sexy. I love that he wants me all the time, even in his sleep.

Knox slides in and out of me, gently, building us up in the most agonizing, delicious way possible. I feel his cock twitch inside of me, making me clench up around him, sucking him in deeper and deeper until he hits the very end of me.

I feel my orgasm blooming up from my core, slowly spreading out to my limbs, making me tremble and cry out softly. It rolls through me, wave after wave seizing my body. It's not as intense as the orgasms he's given me before, but it lasts so long. So, *so* long.

"Breathe for me, love," Knox whispers into my ear before kissing my temple. I gasp for breath and cum again, my release zipping through me like a white-hot flash of lightning. "That's it, angel, God, I'm coming too..."

Knox whispers my name over and over, his head buried in my neck as he pumps his seed into me. He rolls onto his side, holding me close to him while we both catch our breath.

"Why did you seduce me like that, angel? Now you're going to be late for breakfast."

"What?! Me? You! You did this!" I exclaim, hitting him on the chest playfully as I try to twist out of his arms.

"Nope. It was all you. Being naked and gorgeous and right next to me. Irresistible. Temptress. Siren."

I smile shyly at his words. They make me feel powerful and vulnerable at the same time. I'm not sure how that's even possible, but everything about Knox makes me feel that way. Like he's prying me open and consuming all of my secrets and pain while giving me the confidence to heal.

Knox gives me one last chaste kiss on the lips and then reluctantly lets me go.

"I'll be lucky to get cold cereal on the table in time for breakfast," I half-joke. I'm already running fifteen minutes behind schedule and I still need to go to my own cabin and get dressed.

"I'll head up to the main house and get something started. You go get ready, love. Take a warm shower, it'll feel good on your sore muscles."

"If you insist," I sigh dramatically and roll my eyes as if it's *such a burden* to be taken care of by him.

Knox throws on a pair of jeans and a t-shirt, runs his fingers through his hair, and he's practically good to go. Ugh. Guys have it so much easier. He gives me a playful smack on the ass, making me squeal and jump away from him.

"I do insist. I always want the best for you. Now let me take care of my woman," he grumps, feigning annoyance at my resistance.

I'm half-way out the door when Knox grabs me by the hips and spins me around, kissing me deeply and stealing the air right out of my lungs.

"There. Now you can go," he grins, spinning me back around and giving me a little push out onto the front porch.

***

I can't keep the stupid happy grin off of my face all throughout breakfast. Jade takes notice and gives me a knowing smile while we're cleaning up after the guys.

"Soooo...?" she drawls, clearly wanting me to fill her in. I debate not telling her anything for about half a second, and then give in. I've never really had friends, and I won't lie, it feels good to have someone to talk to about this sort of stuff. Not that I've ever had this sort of stuff to talk about before, but still.

"Knox and I are a thing," I blurt out, my cheeks heating up as the words fall out of my mouth.

Jade laughs and rolls her eyes. "Well, duh!" I can't help but laugh with her. "I'm glad it's official now. The man has wanted you since day one."

I try to contain my smile but fail miserably. I think I knew it from the first time he locked eyes on me at the wedding reception, but it's nice to hear someone else confirm my suspicions. "Are you okay with that? Like, is there some rule about employee fraternization or something?" The thought suddenly occurs to me that I overstepped some boundaries. Maybe I'm just looking for ways for this to all fall apart. I can't quite believe it's real.

Jade bursts out laughing. "You do realize my husband is the foreman, right?"

I blush harder and roll my eyes, feeling stupid at my question. Obviously, she doesn't have a problem with it. Jade senses my embarrassment and stops laughing. She puts a hand on my shoulder, urging me to look at her.

"It's a good thing," she assures me. "I was worried Knox was going to move too fast, but it looks like you both got the timing right. I'm so happy you came here, Teagan."

I give her a watery smile, the emotions all too much for me to handle this morning. I'm happy, too. I can't imagine still being in L.A., under my mom's thumb. I can't imagine not knowing Jade or Knox, not having a fulfilling job with people I love. A family.

Before I know what's happening, Jade pulls me into a hug. Having a best friend and a boyfriend is all so much more than I could have ever hoped for.

"Now go on and check on your man. I'll finish cleaning up," she tells me once she releases me from her death-grip hug.

"Are you sure? I'm not trying to skip out on my responsibilities. I'm not one of those women who ignore everyone and everything else in their lives once they have a boyfriend."

"Oh, girl. For one thing, I think he's more than your boyfriend, don't you? And for another thing, I know you're not like that. You've worked really hard, not just around here, but on yourself. I see you growing and improving every day." My stupid eyes burn with tears once again, and this time Jade cries along with me. "Don't you know you can't cry around a pregnant woman?" she teases. I laugh through my tears, and then Jade shoos me off.

Once I'm outside, I decide to take a stroll around the property. I still haven't seen very much of it except for the other night with Knox. Even then, I could hardly focus. Just being around him makes my mind all fuzzy and my body tingly. I thought maybe it would improve once we slept together, but if anything, the feelings have grown more intense. I got wet just sitting next to him at breakfast!

I'm walking past one of the barns when suddenly a hand reaches out and pulls me sideways. Before I can yelp, strong arms wrap around me and the familiar scent of leather and citrus engulfs me. Knox's lips come crashing down on mine, no preamble, no teasing, just intense need and hunger.

I claw at Knox, climbing him like the big, sexy tree he is. He growls and lifts me into the air as I wrap my legs around him. Knox takes a few steps and presses me against the wall, sucking on my neck and grinding his hard length into me.

He rests his forehead on mine, panting for air. I love the way his ragged breath feels on my skin, especially when it's me that made him that way.

"What was that for?" I ask once I'm able to form a sentence.

"I saw you walking and had to have you," he explains as if it's obvious.

"Well, you haven't really *had* me yet," I say in my most seductive voice. I'm not sure I pulled it off, but then I see Knox's eyes turn dark and I feel rather than hear the growl deep in his chest.

He sets me down and spins me around so I have to brace myself against the wall. He flips up my skirt and has my panties down around my ankles in half a second, and then I hear his zipper come down.

"God, angel," he says, his voice low and gravelly, rumbling out of his throat in the most delicious way. Knox grips my ass, a hand on each cheek, prying me apart and sliding his dick through my folds. "This tight ass...your fucking gorgeous body..." His hands slip around to my front, snaking up my shirt so he can grab my breasts and knead them. "Love every inch of you," he murmurs into the back of my neck, bending over and covering my back with his front.

I moan at his confession and push back into him, urging him on. "Get inside me, please," I gasp, the need for him literally making it hard to breathe.

"When you ask so nicely..." he grits out.

Knox gives me a few more torturous strokes before slamming that fat cock inside me in one hard thrust. His hand covers my mouth just in time to catch my scream.

"Goddamn... Fuck, Teagan, I know you're sore, baby, I'm sorry." He holds himself still, his words laced with both pain and need.

I don't know what comes over me, but I grip the hand he has over my mouth and slide it down to my throat. "I want it rough," I whisper. "Fuck me, Knox. Fuck me so hard."

Knox pulls almost all the way out and then roars, spearing me with his cock and tearing me in two as he squeezes my neck. I cum instantly, choking on my orgasm.

"Jesus fucking Christ," he growls, pounding into me over and over. He hits me deeper and deeper each time, spreading me wide open and molding my pussy to fit around his massive dick.

Knox tangles his fingers in my hair and rips my head to the side so he can attack my mouth. I bite his lips and suck his tongue inside of my mouth, needing more of him. All of him. We fuck like that, frenzied and frantic like we need this to survive. I think we just might.

My body tenses and locks up, preparing for another powerful release. I tear my mouth away from his and bite my lips to keep from crying out. I slam my eyes shut and push back into him, once, twice, three times, and then my cunt snaps around him so tightly it almost hurts, but in the best way.

He loops an arm under my hips, holding me up right as my knees give out. He presses his body against mine, crushing me against the wall and fucking me furiously. I keep coming, each rough stroke seemingly sending me higher, pushing me deeper into my pleasure until I'm completely lost in bright light and pure bliss.

I feel Knox explode inside of me, biting down on my shoulder as he cums in powerful waves, again and again, more and more of his release shooting into me until I feel it drip down my thighs.

I'm sweating and shaking, unable to stand on my own when Knox finally pulls out of me.

"Fuck," he breathes out, spinning me around and holding me close. "I've never cum so hard. You're incredible. Are you okay? I know you said you wanted it rough, but God... Did I hurt you?"

He peels me off his chest and tips my head up. I can hardly breathe, let alone form words. "I'm good," I say, my words slightly slurred. I've heard of being dick drunk, but I never thought it would happen to me. Then again, I never thought anyone like Knox would happen to me either.

He chuckles and then tucks himself back into his pants before kneeling down in front of me.

"You're a mess, angel," he muses, staring right at my drenched pussy.

"It's your fault," I tease, though I'm still breathless.

"I guess I'll have to clean it up."

"Wha—"

Before I can even get the word out, Knox laps at my pussy, licking up both of our releases. It's so dirty, so completely filthy...and incredibly hot. I grind my cunt against his face and moan when he squeezes my ass in a bruising grip.

My shaky hands find his head and I pull at his hair, needing to hold on to something to anchor me. I feel his mouth every-fucking-where, lips sucking on my clit, teeth nipping at my folds, tongue thrusting in and out of me, demanding my pleasure, and pulling another orgasm to the surface.

I feel it, right there, so close, almost, right there, right there...

"Knox!" I cry out, not even caring who hears me anymore. The tension breaks all over my body as violent spasms grip my muscles and wring my orgasm from the very depths of me.

"That's it, angel, cum all over my tongue," he grunts, licking me from top to bottom.

"Too...much..." I whimper, tugging at his hair.

With one last long lick of my pussy, he tears his mouth away from me and rests his forehead on my stomach, breathing almost as heavily as I am. I hold him close, overwhelmed with the intimacy of being taken so thoroughly so roughly, and yet so lovingly. I love him. I love Knox so much it hurts.

I'm suddenly hit with the thought of him being thrown from that bull and trampled. It wrecks me, so much so I have to steady myself on Knox's broad shoulders.

"Angel?" he asks, steadying me as he pulls my panties up and stands in front of me.

"Please don't leave me," I blurt out, wrapping my arms around his torso and burying my face into his chest.

"I'm not going anywhere, love," he says in a soft, confused voice while massaging my neck.

"Don't go on your last ride," I whisper. Knox stiffens at my words, dropping his hand from my neck. He grips my shoulders in his hands and holds me at arm's length so he can look me in the eyes.

"I have to. But I promise I'll be okay. Nothing is gonna happen to me, angel. Not when I've finally found you."

"Please," I beg again, even though the determination in his features lets me know he won't listen to me.

"Don't make me choose between you and Anthony," he says quietly.

I can't help the tears that fall. The way he said it made it seem like he wouldn't choose me.

Knox crushes me into his chest again, which somehow makes everything even more painful.

"I'm sorry, angel. Please don't cry. I'm sorry. It'll all be okay, I promise. Do you trust me?"

"But—"

"Do you trust me?" He asks again.

"Knox..."

He cups my face so gently in his large hands, wiping away my tears with his thumbs. "Do you trust me?" he whispers, his eyes searching mine, begging me to let him do this as much as I'm begging him not to.

"I trust you," I breathe out so quietly I'm not even sure I said it out loud.

"Then everything will be okay. You'll see. I'll give you the whole world, love."

"All I want is you."

His whole face softens as he gives me a tentative smile. Knox kisses my forehead, my eyelids, my nose, and finally my lips.

"You have me, Teagan. You have all of me."

But for how long?

Chapter 9

Knox

I'm not sure what wakes me up, but my heart is pounding and it's still dark out. Then my dick twitches and I hear Teagan moaning as she rubs her bare ass against my growing shaft. Fuck yes, my woman is insatiable, and I love every second.

My hand glides up her side, following the curve of her hip and the dip in her waist. Teagan whispers her encouragement, whimpering when I squeeze her breast and grind my cock in between her cheeks.

"Need me to take care of you, angel?" I murmur, my voice raspy with sleep. I let my hand slide down her torso and dip in between her folds, collecting her sweet honey before plunging two fingers deep inside of her.

"Yes," she gasps, rocking her hips into my hand. I can hear how desperate she is, how much she needs me in this most basic way.

I withdraw my hand and pump my cock a few times, getting myself all nice and slick with her juices. I grip her thigh and bring her leg back so it's draping over mine, opening her up for me so I can sink into her while we're spooning like this.

She's so fucking tight like this. I have to open her up with shallow thrusts until her pussy stretches and swallows me whole.

"Knox, ohmygod, oh God, you're so..." She cries out before finishing her thought, letting me know I found her G-spot.

"That's it, love, feel me, all of me. This ripe, juicy cunt is mine, your orgasms are mine, your laughter, your tears, all of you is mine, Teagan," I grit out as I thrust into her in long, hard strokes.

I kiss up and down her neck, nipping and sucking on her tender skin until I feel her tremble in my arms. Reaching down, I play with her clit, pinching it between my fingers right as I slam into her roughly.

Again, and again I hammer into her and roll her little ball of nerves between my thumb and pointer finger. Her walls flutter around me and her back arches away from me, even as I hold her close.

"Cum for me, angel. Make this pussy pop," I grunt into her ear. She whimpers as I hold her close and fuck into that tight, wet little hole, ripping her open and demanding her orgasm.

I can't stop my own release from tightening my balls and shooting out of my aching, raw cock. Teagan clenches around me and lets out a broken cry as we cum together. She pitches forward and curls in on herself, her tiny body shaking as she wraps her arms around her torso and folds herself into a ball.

"Teagan? Are you okay, angel?" I smirk to myself a little as I roll over and pull her into my arms, thinking that I've just given her an amazing orgasm that she needs time to recover from.

To my horror, when I turn her over to face me, she has tears in her eyes. I'm completely gutted, the thought of hurting her makes me sick to my stomach.

"Please don't go," she begs me through her tears.

I take a deep breath, sighing in relief that she's okay, at least physically. I hold her close, rocking her back and forth. I'm leaving in a few hours to go to the rodeo in El Paso. We haven't talked about it since that day in the barn. We've been in our own little bubble these last two weeks. A perfect paradise of laughter, walks around the ranch, late nights in bed, and snuggling up by the fire. We knew this day was coming, but we chose to ignore it.

I had hoped her anxiety about the whole thing would ease up as she became more secure in who we are together. I should have talked to her about it before now, but I didn't know what to say. How else can I express to her what this means to me? It isn't just about Anthony anymore, it's about Teagan as well.

Everything is all wrapped up in this last ride. I feel like once I ride out my eight seconds on Tank, I'll finally be able to lay Anthony down to rest for good. I'll prove to Teagan I'm a man who doesn't back down from a challeng. I'm a man who can take on her past, her pain, her insecurities and anxieties. I'll show her I'm a man of my word, that I'll honor Anthony's dying wish, that I'll honor every promise I make to her, including our wedding vows.

"Come with me," I whisper into her hair, kissing the top of her head.

Teagan jerks away from me and looks at me like I've lost my mind. "Are you serious? How can you even ask me that? If you're going to kill yourself, then I'm not going to be there to witness it."

"Wait, love—"

"No!" she yells, rolling off of the bed and taking the sheet with her so she can cover herself up. I hate that she's hiding her beautiful body from me. Teagan grips the sheet like it's a shield that can protect her from...what? Me?

"Teagan, just let me—"

"No, Knox. I can't. I can't..." she wipes tears from her eyes and turns on her heel towards the small bathroom.

I leap out of bed and follow her, trying to think of something to say, anything at all, that will ease her worry and make her confident in me. In us.

The bathroom door slams in my face, the lock clicking a split second later.

"Angel, please..." I sigh defeatedly, resting my forehead on the cheap, flimsy bathroom door. I could break it down easily, but I won't violate her space like that.

"I can't look at you right now," she says angrily, though I can tell she's fighting back tears. "You said not to make you choose, so I'm not. I'll be here, Knox, waiting for you. I just wish you wouldn't do this. Please, please don't do this."

"I have to," I say weakly. "I know you don't understand. You just have to trust me. That's all I've ever asked of you." There's silence on the other side of the door, and then muffled sobs, as if she's crying into the sheet that was draped around her body. We stand there, on either side of the locked door, silently begging each other to cave. It's torture. I know she thinks this is my fault, but she's making an issue where there doesn't need to be one. I don't know how to tell her that without coming off as an asshole. So, I don't say anything at all.

"If you're going off to the rodeo, then go. Now. Leave, Knox. When I get out of the shower, I don't want you here. It'll be too hard," she bites out.

"I don't have to leave for another few hours—"

"You don't *have* to leave *at all*!" she yells. I can feel the fear and fury radiating off her. I hate that I'm the one who caused it. I know deep down that I can take it all away if I go fight my demons, ride the fucking bull, and come back. I'll take all her hurt and anger away. I just have to do this one thing.

"I love you," I tell her for the first time. I've loved her since the moment I saw her, but I haven't put it into words until right now. I had hoped it would be under better circumstances, but I need her to know where I stand so she doesn't think I'm abandoning her. I'm doing this for her, for us.

"Please just leave," she whispers.

Fuck, it hurts. I know she's just scared. I know she wants me here, hell, I know she *loves* me. But she's letting her fear take control. That's okay. I'll take on her fear. I'll carry it with me, I'll ride out the storm, and come back to her unscathed.

The shower turns on, letting me know Teagan is done with this conversation. I step back from the door and get dressed. We're both hurting. We're both raw. I'll give her this space, even though it pains me.

Trudging towards the door of her cabin, I look back to the bathroom where I know she's standing in the shower, crying. I have a split second of indecision. Just one flicker of doubt.

But I shut that shit down and put on my game face. Two days. I'll be back in two days.

***

I haven't talked to Teagan in fourteen hours. Fourteen. Fucking. Hours. I'm miserable. I hate how we left things. I made it to the hotel in El Paso a few hours ago. I don't have to be anywhere until tomorrow, but they always want us to check in early. There are a few gimmicky radio spots and photo ops my manager wants me to do later tonight, but right now, I'm alone in my room, missing Teagan with every cell in my body.

I've called her a few times and sent her several texts, but of course she's not answering me. I know she's upset, but God, I just want to hear her voice. Even if she's yelling at me.

I rub my eyes and look at the clock on the nightstand for the hundredth time this hour. It's just after five-thirty. Teagan is probably getting dinner ready. I hope Jade is with her. Those two have become fast friends, and I've never been more grateful for the family Teagan and I have found at Rivera Ranch.

"Fuck," I grumble when I pull my hand away from my eyes and see wetness there. I'm crying. Fucking crying. This is the absolute worst state of mind to be in the night before a big event. I shake my head back and forth and decide to go take a shower and then head over to the rodeo. Might as well occupy my mind with something else for a while. I'll be back with Teagan soon.

Twenty minutes later, I'm toweling off and rummaging through my overnight back for a fresh t-shirt. I pull it on and grab my keys and my phone, getting ready to head out for the evening. I look at my phone, hoping beyond hope Teagan called. Instead, I see I have two missed calls from Noah and one from Jade.

I call Noah back, thinking maybe I forgot to finish something before leaving. I probably did, seeing as I was in a terrible mood all day.

"Knox, is Teagan with you?" Noah demands. Fear and adrenaline spike through my veins.

No. Fuck, no. Did she run away?

"No," I grit out, trying to swallow back the bile creeping up my throat.

"When is the last time you saw her?"

"This morning," I croak. "Early. Before breakfast."

"Goddamnit," Noah growls, though it's a faded sound like he pulled the phone away from him. I hear Jade whimper something in the background.

"What's happening? Where is she?" I'm pacing around the room, clenching my fists in an attempt not to put one through the fucking wall.

"She left for the grocery store around ten this morning. We haven't seen her since."

"Fuck!" I roar, kicking a chair over. "What can I do? I'm coming back. No, wait, I'm already this much closer to L.A., I'll drive there. Right now. I'm leaving," I ramble almost manically into the phone.

"Now hold on a goddamn minute. I don't know how to tell you this..."

"Tell me," I growl, my fist tightening so much that I feel my nails bite into my palm and draw blood. Good. The pain is the only thing keeping me grounded right now.

"The truck she drove is still in the grocery store parking lot. We got a call half an hour ago from an employee there who recognized it as one of ours. Looks like she was half-way through loading the groceries inside before..."

He doesn't finish the thought, but he doesn't have to. She didn't run. She was kidnapped. I throw the phone down on the bed before I snap it in my fist. I smash my fist down on the desk in the corner of the room, splintering the wood. I'll buy a new one, I don't give a fuck. Nothing matters. Nothing but finding her.

Noah barks through the phone, so I pick it up again and resume my pacing.

"We got the cops looking for her, Jacob, Isaiah, Cory, Zane, we're all out looking for her. Do you think—"

"Her mom," I cut him off, finishing his thought. "It has to be her mom. Fuck. I didn't even think...I just assumed Teagan made a clean break, but..."

"We all did. There's no time for regret right now, we need action. Measured and controlled action," Noah says pointedly. "No flying off the handle. So calm the fuck down and start heading this way. If it's her mom taking her back to L.A., they have about a six-hour head start, according to some clues the cops picked up on. People are saying they spotted an orange hybrid SUV type thing creeping around town lately, especially around the grocery store. You keep heading out east, they'll be heading west. It's a long shot, especially assuming they're taking main highways, but I think that's what you need to do right now. If you get back here and you haven't spotted them, we'll regroup back here at the ranch, okay? The highway patrol is on this too. We're all on this. We're going to find her, Knox."

I grunt something in response, I'm not sure what, and then hang up.

I shouldn't have left her. I shouldn't have fucking left her. I broke my promise to her. I already hurt her.

I pray that she can somehow forgive me when I find her. And I *will* fucking find her.

Chapter 10

Teagan

Pain explodes on the side of my head and my eyes fly open. I'm in the dark and I'm...moving? I try sitting up but find that I'm all folded up in some small space. I try to breathe through the panic and pain enough to figure out how I got here. Wherever *here* is.

My mind is all fuzzy. I keep forming thoughts, but they vanish like smoke before I can capture them. There's rumbling all around me, the container I'm in is jostling back and forth. I try taking a few more deep breaths as the world around me starts to come into focus.

I'm in a trunk.

My head smacks against the floor as we go over a pothole. That must have been what woke me up.

I lie still and take a quick inventory of my body now that I'm a little more awake. I don't feel any major injuries, aside from my now throbbing head, and I'm not tied up.

The last thing I remember is going to the grocery store. It hurt like hell that Knox wasn't with me. Tuesdays are his days off and he's been using them to go grocery shopping with me. The first time he offered to come, he said it was just convenient since he needed to pick a few things up for himself. Even back then I knew it was a flimsy excuse. He really came along because he knew crowds and new places scared me. It's one more way he was taking care of me until I messed it all up.

Tears sting my eyes when I think about the last thing I said to him. *Please just leave.*

I banished him after he told me he loved me. I regretted the words as soon as they left my mouth, but I was too hurt, too scared, too stubborn to take them back. I should have gone with him. It would have been awful to be in the stadium with a mass of people around me, but I should have done it. I love him too, so much, and now he might never know. After everything he's done for me, all of the ways he's shown me love and earned my trust, I couldn't find it in me to show my support for the biggest ride of his life.

I brace myself as we go over another pothole, the movement jarring me out of my downward spiral and allowing me to get back to the task at hand - remembering how the fuck I got here.

I was moping around the grocery store, battling feelings of betrayal, guilt, and abandonment. It's not a fun combination. Zero out of ten, would not recommend. I think I got everything on the list. I remember talking to the cashier. And then loading up the truck...

Wait. No.

My mom. Her shrill laugh. Her long fake nails clawing at my arm. Oscar telling my mom not to damage the merchandise, aka, me. It's something he said a lot whenever my mom would get aggressive.

Don't grab her so hard, she's got a commercial for Maybelline tomorrow. Can't have you damaging the merchandise.

Instead of fear, anger churns in my gut. I'm not merchandise. I'm not a thing. I'm not a pawn to be used in their sick game. I have value beyond my looks, beyond the money I can make. I'm worthy of more than that shallow life.

I know my surge of confidence is all thanks to Knox. More guilt pierces me thinking about how I screwed everything up.

My mom loosened her grip and then Oscar put a rag over my face. The last thing I remember is his smooth, snake-like voice slithering into my ear. "Welcome back, little darling. You've been a very bad girl. I'll show you how you can make it up to me when we get back home."

The words twist around in my head and then lodge themselves in my throat, making it hard to breathe. Oscar was always a creeper, but he never crossed that line. Then again, I haven't spent any time around him since my eighteenth birthday. Maybe that's all the permission he needs.

I can't go back there. I won't survive. Especially now that I know what it means to be loved and accepted. Not just by Knox, but Jade,

Noah, hell, everyone at Rivera Ranch. The only family I've ever had. I have to get back to them, to Knox. I have to apologize, to tell him I love him.

The car slows down and then turns before coming to a stop. We idle for a few moments, and then the car shuts off. My heart is thudding painfully in my chest as I begin to shake. What do they have planned for me? Where did we stop? Surely, they didn't drive all the way back to L.A. already. I couldn't have been out that long.

"Wait!" I hear my mom call out to Oscar. "What about..." I assume she's motioning towards the trunk, asking Oscar what to do about me while they go off and do whatever they need to do.

"She'll be out cold for a few more hours, it's fine."

"Are you sure? One of us should stay in the car with her, don't you think?"

"It'd look weird if we went into the rest stop individually. We can't afford to look out of place."

My mom sighs dramatically. It's a sound I'm all too familiar with. Cue the eye roll. "Why couldn't we have taken a plane, again? It's a long fucking drive from Bumfuck, Texas to L.A.," she whines, sounding like a spoiled child. I guess she kind of is.

"Seriously, woman? How do you suppose we would have gotten Teagan on board? She would have pitched a fit. This is the only way."

Mom grumbles something, the sound fading away, along with their footsteps.

This is my chance. I'm not tied up, probably thanks to Oscar's "not damaging the property" policy, and we're at a rest stop, which means they have to have workers and other people around. I just need to get out of the car.

I blindly feel my way around the trunk, hoping to find a tire iron or something so I can break out of here, or at the very least alert someone to the fact that I'm in here.

I don't find a tire iron. I find something a million times better.

The release latch for the back seat. The fold-down back seats were one of the selling points for this car. The dumb bitch is driving *my* Ford Escape. I giggle to myself at the name. God, I must still be feeling the effects of whatever Oscar used to knock me out. I shouldn't be laughing at a time like this, but I can't help it.

I raise a shaky hand and smooth my fingers over the hidden latch. I can do this. I need to act right now. I need to squeeze myself out into the back seat, get out of the car, and run for my fucking life. I need to do it right now.

Right now, Dammit!

I know all of this, but anxiety halts my progress. What if they come back before I can get out? Will it make my punishment worse? What if no one believes me? What if I get out of the car and tell someone, but my mom and Oscar call me crazy and then have me committed? That last one sounds outrageous, but honestly, I wouldn't put it past those two.

"Come on, you can do this, you can do this," I mutter to myself.

Knox's words from that morning I spilled my guts to him fill my head.

Being brave doesn't mean you're not afraid. It means you're scared shitless. And then you do the damn thing anyway.

"Do the damn thing, Teagan," I tell myself more forcefully.

And then I do.

The latch clicks, the seat bends forward, and I shove myself out of the trunk before opening the back door and slinking out. I take a quick peek around to see if I can spot mom or Oscar, but I don't see them anywhere. I quickly put the seat back and close the door. If I play my cards right, they might not even notice I'm gone until the next stop.

My head is spinning, and the ground is tilting beneath my wobbly steps, but I manage to orient myself enough to see I'm at a large gas station. It's one of those that have regular pumps with gas, and then larger, sectioned off areas with wide diesel pumps for semi-trucks.

I duck and weave behind the other cars, making my way to the eighteen-wheelers. My half thought out plan is to hide behind a truck until I'm sure mom and Oscar have left. I settle for a nondescript, white semi with no identifying logos. It has a plain black cab, unlike some of the others that have bright colors or decals on the hood.

Taking one last look around the parking lot, I dart out from my current hiding spot behind a green Prius and run straight for the truck. I only take a breath once my back is pressed against the cool metal of the semi.

I'm trembling from head to toe, my stomach is rolling, and my head is throbbing so much I can barely hear anything around me.

But I did it. I got out.

"You okay there, little miss?" A deep voice jerks me from my small moment of victory. A chill runs down my spine as I think about how this might not have been the best plan. I'm a small woman, still half-drugged, and now I'm practically throwing myself at a bunch of truckers. Shit.

I pry one eye open and see a large man with a full grey beard and kind blue eyes. He's probably in his sixties, and he doesn't look threatening at all. In fact, he looks like a concerned grandpa.

I nod my head but then wince against the vertigo caused by the movement.

"Take it easy now," the man says, his voice soft and calming. "You're okay right here, little lady. Can I call someone for you? Actually, here, you can take my phone." He unlocks it for me and hands it over.

I take it in my shaking hands and dig through my mind for Knox's phone number. Everything is jumbled up and I feel like I'm going to pass out. Fuck. I'm so close to freedom. So close.

"Can I look something up for you, maybe? A business or a public number that might be listed?" My savior asks.

"R-ranch," I stutter out, handing him the phone back. "Rivera Ranch."

The man taps the screen a few times and pulls up the website, flashing me the screen to confirm it's the right place. I nod and then wince again.

"Here ya go, miss. It's ringing."

He places the phone in my hand, and I bring it up to my ear.

One ring.

Two rings.

"Rivera Ranch, I have to call you back, we're going through a bit of a—"

"Jade?" I rasp out, cutting her off.

"Oh my God, Teagan?" she practically yells. I pull the phone back, trying to put some distance between myself and her piercing voice. "Are you okay? Where are you? We're so worried. Oh my God, Noah! Noah, it's Teagan!" she yells again.

"I'm at a truck stop…" I look up at the man who is keeping his distance, trying to give me my space.

"We're just outside of Fort Stockton, on highway ten," he supplies before I can ask.

I repeat the information to Jade, who repeats it to Noah.

"Okay, hun, Noah is talking to Knox on the phone right now. Knox is on his way from El Paso, he's about an hour away. Are you safe? Can you… Oh, just a sec." There's mumbling in the background. "Okay, hang on, Teagan. Knox is on his way. The cops know where you are, there's probably going to be a highway patrol car coming your way. You'll be safe with them. Knox will pick you up at the station in Fort Stockton, okay?"

"Yeah," I manage to squeak out through tears. It's only been a few hours, but I already miss Jade and the ranch more than I thought possible. Hearing her voice, knowing I'm close to being home, and yet so far still, it all hits me at once. I'm a sobbing mess. The poor truck driver digs around in his pocket and hands me a cloth tissue. It's very sweet and old-fashioned and makes me cry even harder. Jade tries to console me, so I suck it up enough to tell her goodbye.

Just then, two patrol vehicles pull in across the parking lot. The kind stranger quirks an eyebrow up and gives me a slight nod of his head. I know he's asking if I want them to find me or if I want to stay hidden. In this moment, I swear I could kiss the man. I don't, obviously, but his kindness and loyalty are incredible.

"That's my ride," I tell him with a smile so he knows it's okay. He waves them down, and before I know it, I'm covered in a blanket and someone is handing me a bottle of water.

I close my eyes for a second, and when I open them back up, I'm in the back of the cop car. I blink, and I'm at the station. I blink again, and I'm surrounded by fluorescent lights and the steady beeping of monitors.

My eyes are dry and my limbs are heavy. I try telling the nurse checking my vitals that my cowboy is coming to save me, but I don't think she hears me. She just gives me a sad smile and tells me to get some rest. I don't have it in me to argue. Maybe the next time I open my eyes I'll be in my warm bed with Knox and this will all have been a horrible nightmare.

Chapter 11

Knox

"Nnnooo...I need...Knox. KNOX!"

"Shh, angel, I'm right here, I'm right here, love," I murmur against Teagan's forehead before pressing my lips to her warm skin. She mumbles something and curls up even further into my chest as I tighten my arms around her.

Fucking hell, she's okay. I have her here in my arms. I still can't believe it. I broke dozens of traffic laws on my way to Fort Stockton in an attempt to get to my angel as quickly as possible. I showed up at the police station like Noah told me to, only to discover Teagan was taken to the hospital after passing out. My heart dropped to the floor and splintered into a million pieces at the thought of her being hurt so badly she needed medical care.

I was able to get a police escort to the hospital, probably because the cop I talked to wisely assumed I'd continue to break traffic laws with or without the escort, so they might as well lead the charge. At first, the nurses weren't going to let me see Teagan, but I told them I was her fiancée. That will be true soon enough.

The nurse comes in to check on Teagan and gives me a sharp look, probably because I climbed into the hospital bed and wrapped myself up in Teagan as soon as I stepped into the room two hours ago and haven't left.

The doctor informed me that she's doing really well, there are no major injuries or health concerns. She's dehydrated and has a nasty bump on her head, but other than that she's mostly just sleeping off the chloroform her mom used to knock her out. I tighten my fists at the thought of anyone harming Teagan, let alone her own flesh and blood, but I quickly let that go for now. Even though she's asleep, Teagan seems to know when I'm tense. It makes her tense, too, like we're connected on some deep level.

Teagan wakes up every now and then, usually calling out for me or crying, sometimes even kicking or lashing out as if she's still trying to escape. It fucking tears me in two, but she instantly calms down when I talk to her and remind her I'm here.

My back hurts like a motherfucker from trying to squeeze my too-tall frame into this bed, and I'm impossibly exhausted, but I'll stay here forever if it means I can provide comfort for my angel and reassure her I'm not leaving her.

She stirs in my arms and tilts her head up, blinking at me sleepily. My heart stops in my chest. It's the first time she's opened her eyes. I see fear, confusion, and finally, relief.

"Knox?" she whispers. "Are you really here?" Her voice catches in her throat as tears form and fall from her beautiful blue eyes.

"I'm here, love. I've got you. You're gonna be okay now," I tell her, wiping away her tears.

"Oh my God, Knox," she cries, clutching my shirt in her tiny fists and pulling me closer. "You're okay? You didn't get hurt?"

I furrow my brow in confusion, thinking maybe she's still a little dazed from her deep sleep and the drugs. But then I realize she must think I went on my last ride before coming to her. My sweet angel. Worried about me even though she was fucking kidnapped.

"I'm fine. I left before my event, I had to get to you." I'm expecting relief to fill her eyes, but to my horror, she looks ashamed.

"Please don't hate me," she whimpers. Fuck, my heart is in my damn throat at her words.

"Hate you? No, love, never. Why would I hate you?"

"I made you miss the most important thing. I didn't support you, I should have come with you, I'm so sorry, Knox, I—"

I cut her off with a soft kiss on her lips. God, I can't stand the thought of her feeling guilty about any of this. "Please don't apologize, Teagan. Not about this. Nothing is your fault, do you understand? I never should have left you. I knew how upset and anxious you were, and fuck, I made you doubt us. Made you doubt that *you*, love, only you are the most important thing."

"But what about—"

"Nothing else matters. I'm nothing without you. And to think I could have lost you today..."

It's Teagan's turn to cut me off with a kiss.

"I'm right here."

"Thank fuck," I sigh, tucking her head back into my chest. "I love you, angel."

Teagan sniffles into my shirt, and then turns her head to place a sweet kiss over my heart. I just about break and cry along with her, but I have to keep it together for her right now. "I love you too, Knox. So much."

Our sweet moment is interrupted by a light knock on the door, and then two police officers file into the room.

"Ma'am, is it a good time to take your statement? We only got the names of your kidnappers before you fainted," the officer says quietly.

I reluctantly loosen my hold on Teagan and help her readjust so she's facing the officers. Her back is to my front, and I have my arms wrapped around her waist. I need to be touching her at all times. That's non-negotiable.

"I'm ready," Teagan says with confidence and fierceness in her voice. I'm so damn proud of her for taking this head-on.

The officer nods and pulls out some paperwork and a pen. "Can you tell us what you remember about when you were taken and how you escaped?"

Teagan takes a deep breath and I squeeze her gently to let her know I'm here with her all the way. She explains being in the parking lot, her mom and Oscar taking her, waking up in the trunk of her own car at the rest stop, and then cleverly escaping.

She turns and looks at me over her shoulder, smiling softly. God, I don't deserve her love after what I put her through, but I need it all the same. "I remembered what you told me when you first came to the ranch," she whispers so only I can hear. "About being brave and scared and doing the damn thing anyway. See? You did save me after all."

Fuck it. I lean forward and kiss her with everything I have. We only break apart when one of the officers clears their throats.

"We have your mother and Oscar in custody. They will be charged with first-degree kidnapping, which is a class A felony. I probably shouldn't discuss it with you just yet, but I can't imagine a jury that wouldn't convict those two after we get the footage from the rest stop of you climbing out of the car. Plus, we talked to Henry Appleton, who was the gentleman who let you use his phone. With his testimony, those two are as good as gone."

"Henry? Do you have his contact information? I'd like to thank him," Teagan says.

"Actually, he's out in the waiting room, would you like me to send him in when we're done?"

"Yes, please," Teagan nods eagerly.

A few minutes later, the officers leave and a portly older gentleman with a grey beard walks in. He sizes me up as if deciding if I'm a safe person. I'm forever grateful for his kindness and his protectiveness towards my angel, and this is one more way he's looking out for her.

Henry must find me worthy because he turns his attention towards Teagan. He smiles broadly at her, his eyes full of compassion.

"I sure am glad to see you're doing better, little miss," he says warmly.

"I'm Teagan," she says, offering her hand for him to shake. He grasps it delicately and introduces himself as well. "I can't thank you enough for helping me. You saved my life," she says, a shudder running through her tiny body. I kiss her temple and run my hands up and down her arms in a soothing gesture.

"I just did what I hope any decent person would do. My granddaughter is about your age. I can't imagine her being scared and all alone. I'm just glad I was at the right place at the right time," he says humbly.

"How can we repay you?" I ask, speaking for the first time since he entered the room.

"Oh, please, no need for that. Seeing Teagan on the mend is all I need."

I offer my hand for him to shake, which he does. "I'm Knox, by the way. I can't thank you enough for being there for my girl. If anything ever happened to her..."

"No need to worry about that now, son," he assures me. "You just take good care of her."

"Always," I say with all the conviction in my heart.

***

"Hey, angel, are you ready to get out of here?" I ask Teagan once she wakes up from another nap. The doctor came in about twenty minutes ago and said she could leave whenever she woke up. He gave me instructions for her care and things to look out for, and I promised to bring her back if anything seemed worrisome.

"Hell yes," she mumbles, a cute little grin playing at her lips.

"God, I love you," I whisper before kissing the smile right off of her face.

"Love you too," she says, her cheeks flushed my favorite color of pink. Well, my second favorite. Her pretty pink pussy is number one on my list.

"Let's get out of here. I booked a hotel for us tonight so we won't have to make the drive back to the ranch just yet. We can get you cleaned up and a good night's sleep under your belt before hitting the road, okay?"

"Sounds perfect."

Half an hour later, I'm unlocking the door to our room. Teagan still looks exhausted, but she's got some of her color back and a smile on her face. She's so strong and incredible. I can't believe she's mine. All mine.

"Do you want to take a hot shower, love? I can order some food to be delivered when you get out."

"Mmm..." She taps her chin and gives me a saucy look. "How about you join me?"

I groan and cup her cheek, kissing her lightly on the forehead. "As much as I want that, I don't think you're up for any physical activities right now," I murmur into her ear.

She tsks at me and leans back to look me in the eyes. "Is sex the only thing you think about?" she teases, tossing my words back at me from our very first encounter.

"When it comes to you? It's definitely up there. But I also think about how amazing, kind, and hardworking you are. You're kind of the whole package, angel."

She smiles at me, but then she looks away, dipping her head down as if she's shy. "Do you think...maybe you could just..." she sighs and shakes her head. I grip her chin lightly and tip her face up so she's looking right at me.

"What is it?"

"I just want to be near you. I know it's crazy, but you being in a different room than me feels too far away."

I wrap Teagan up in my embrace and rock her gently back and forth. "Of course, love. It's not crazy. I feel the same way, but I didn't want to crowd you."

"Crowd me, please crowd me," she giggles. I grin and kiss the top of her head before leading us to the bathroom.

Stripping her down, I notice little scratches and bruises on her delicate skin, probably from being tossed in a trunk and rattled around for hours on end. Thinking about it is pissing me off, so I have to close my eyes and take a deep breath. I feel Teagan's soft little hand stroke my cheek, making me open my eyes and look up at her from my position on the floor after I slipped her pants and panties off.

"I'm okay," she whispers. "And you're okay. That's all that matters."

I nod and stand up, turning the water on and stripping out of my own clothes. Teagan runs her hands up and down my chest and stomach, not sexually, but more like she's testing to see if I'm real. I gather her hands up in mine and kiss one palm and then the other.

Leading us over to the shower, I make sure the water is hot before we step in. Once inside, Teagan turns to me and kisses my chest, burying her face there and breathing me in.

"I love the way you smell. Like leather and grass and citrus," she whispers.

I chuckle and reach for the little bottle of body soap provided by the hotel, pouring some in my hand and rubbing her back and arms while holding her. "I love the way you smell too, angel. Like crisp apples and honey."

"I love the way you feel. Hard and warm and like *mine*."

I spin Teagan around, pressing her back to my front so I can wash up her chest and torso. Bending down, I nip at her neck and graze my lips over the shell of her ear. "I love the way you feel, too. Soft and silky and like *home*."

She sighs and leans into me, letting me hold up her weight while I continue to scrub the terrible day off her. "I love how you make me feel precious and cared for. I've never truly mattered to anyone before, but I matter to you. You make me feel so loved."

God, her words are every fucking thing to me. "I'll be right back, angel," tell her before hopping out of the shower. She looks adorably confused. Ten seconds later, I join her again, getting down on one knee and taking her left hand in mine. Her eyes go wide and fill with tears, but there's a tentative smile on her lips.

"Teagan, you are so very loved. You matter. You are my whole goddamn world, angel, have been since I first laid eyes on you. I know this isn't the traditional proposal, but nothing about us has been traditional. You make me feel so damn vulnerable, so I guess kneeling in front of you completely naked is appropriate," I wink at her. "I can't stand another second going by without you having my ring on your finger. I pray to God you already have my baby in your belly, but if not, we'll just keep trying." She giggles through her tears, the sight making my heart clench up tight. I slip the diamond ring on her trembling finger and kiss it. "I bought this the day after we met. I knew it then, and I'm even more sure of it now, you're my forever. Love you so much, Teagan, so fucking much."

She sniffles and runs her fingers through my hair. I close my eyes and let her touch calm me down.

"Are you going to ask me or...?"

I pop one eye open and melt for her when I see the playful smirk on her face. "I did say this wasn't a traditional proposal. In fact, it's more like me telling you what our plans are going to be for the next eighty years."

"Oh?" She bites her lips and tugs at my hair to get me to stand up. "And what are those plans, exactly?" Teagan presses her curvy little body into me, resting her chin on my chest and looking up into my eyes.

"Well first, we're going to get married as soon as possible. Then we're going to get started on a family right away. We can stay at Rivera Ranch or we can buy our own land nearby. I'm going to spoil you every single moment of every day. You'll always know how cherished you are, how beautiful, how brave, how *mine* you are. I'll love you till the end of time. The rest we'll figure out along the way. How does that sound?"

I kiss the tip of her nose and run my hands up and down her back.

"That sounds like a dream come true," she sighs, stretching up on her toes to kiss the side of my neck.

"Not a dream, angel. It's our reality. Starting right now."

She smiles at me, those bright blue eyes sparkling with so much love it's overwhelming.

"Yes, please," Teagan whispers, kissing me softly on the lips.

"Anything for you," I vow, kissing her right back.

"Mmm... Careful what you wish for," she teases.

"You're everything I've ever wished for, angel."

"You too, Knox. My relentless cowboy."

Epilogue

Teagan

Knox pulls my hair and spanks my ass, tearing into me from behind, riding me hard.

"You like that, baby? Like when I fuck you rough and dirty?" he grits out, moving his hands to my hips and digging his fingers in. Knox bounces me off his cock, hitting home with each powerful stroke.

"Y-yes," I whimper, followed by a loud cry when he cracks his hand over my ass again.

"Fuck, I like it too, angel." Knox licks the sweat off the side of my neck and bites me there, I jerk my hips and clamp my pussy down on him, loving the pain he brings with my pleasure.

I've already cum twice, and my thighs are a sticky mess, but Knox shows me no mercy. I'm so swollen and sensitive that each thrust sparks my nerves deliciously, keeping me right on the edge, so close, more, harder, deeper, again, again...

"I feel you, love, I feel you, fuck... Let go for me, I've got you."

He hammers in and out of me, grunting each time his cock bumps up against my womb. My breath comes out in shallow bursts and then stops altogether when my body tenses and squeezes up tight. All at once, the tension is released as a great wave washes over me and carries me under. I spasm around his huge dick again and again, my limbs shaking and my arms giving out.

Knox holds me up and pumps into me once, twice, three times, and then roars his own climax. I feel his cum shoot into me in forceful bursts. We're both panting and sweating, trembling as our orgasms slowly fade. Every single time with Knox is amazing.

"Well, that's one way to christen the new cabin," Knox laughs as he scoops my limp body up in his arms and gets us settled on the couch, wrapping a blanket around our naked bodies.

"I would argue that it's the best way," I murmur, basking in the afterglow. I feel more than hear the deep chuckle that bubbles out of his chest.

These last six months have been crazy in the best way possible. Jade practically shoved Knox out of the way when we got back to the ranch after the whole mess with my mom and Oscar. She hugged me so tightly I could barely breathe. I sobbed in her arms while she sobbed in mine. I still can't believe I found this place, found my family. It's more than anything I could have ever hoped for myself.

Knox and I got married a month after he proposed. Our wedding was the second event to be held at Rivera Ranch, and it was perfect. We decided to stay on at the ranch, on the condition that we could build our own cabin a bit farther away from everyone else.

Noah and Jade were only too happy to oblige and even offered to pay for it, seeing as having another four-bedroom house would increase the property value. Knox wasn't having any of that, of course. He did accept help from Noah and the rest of the guys to build the cabin. Jade and I helped out when we could, but Jade was very pregnant during most of the construction and had her baby two weeks ago.

Little Aria is so adorable and precious I can hardly stand it. Knox and I have been trying for a while to get pregnant and I was getting really discouraged that it hadn't happened yet. Until today, that is. Well, I mean it happened a while ago, but I got the results today. Knox doesn't know I went to the doctor to confirm this morning while he and the guys moved in what little furniture we have.

"What are you thinking about?" Knox whispers, stroking my back in calming circles.

I smile against his chest and turn my head to kiss him there. "Decorating our new home, of course," I reply.

"Oh yeah? And what are your plans, angel?"

I push myself up a bit on his chest so we're eye-to-eye. God, his beautiful grey eyes get me every single time. I can't believe this incredibly sexy, impossibly kind man is all mine. Forever.

"Love?" he asks, a little smirk playing on his soft lips like he knows exactly what distracted me.

I bite my lip in an attempt to hold back my smile, but judging by the sparkle in his eyes, it didn't work. "I was thinking we'll need a sturdy four-poster bed, for obvious reasons."

Knox grins and nips at my jaw playfully. "What else?"

"Oh, you know. A crib, a bassinet, a changing table, and one of those comfy gliding rocker things for when the baby won't stop crying all night and you have to stay up with him or her. I'll need my beauty rest, of course," I wink at Knox.

His entire face is frozen in shock, almost as if his brain needs to catch up with what he just heard. "Crib? Baby?" he stutters out. He's completely adorable. I make a mental note to surprise him more often if he's going to give me cute, sexy looks like this.

I nod in confirmation. "And the rocking chair. Don't forget the rocking chair."

"For when I'm holding our baby," he says quietly, still a little dazed from the news.

"Yup. Our little baby that I'm growing in my belly right now. Little bean is about six weeks along."

"Oh my God, Teagan," he whispers, his eyes growing glassy. "This is the best news. I can't... God, angel, I'm so fucking happy," Knox says before cupping my face in his hands and pulling me forward so he can kiss me deeply. In one quick, yet careful move, he rolls us so I'm on my back on the couch. Knox kisses down my body and nuzzles into my belly.

"I was worried it wouldn't happen," I confess. "I thought maybe I was broken."

Knox gives my non-existent baby bump one last kiss and then crawls back up my body to rest his forehead on mine. "You're not broken, Teagan. Even if you couldn't get pregnant, you wouldn't be broken. You're fucking perfect and you're mine. Both of you. I will love you with everything I am, protect you with everything that I have."

"You already do," I say kissing him lightly on the lips.

"Well, get ready for me to turn it up a notch. I'm talking overprotective, dedicated, obsessed husband here."

"Hmm... and what does that entail?" I ask, resting my head down on his shoulder and tracing patterns over the warm, smooth skin of his chest.

"For starters, I'm taking over breakfast duty. You're sleeping in." I open my mouth to protest but Knox plows on, letting me know how it's going to be. I don't really mind, and in fact I kind of like him taking charge. But I have to put up a fight every now and then just to show him I can. "Foot rubs every night. Several orgasms a day. To relax you, of course."

"Of course," I nod, giggling when he pinches my ass.

"I'll think of more. Don't you worry. You're going to be so pampered, like the goddess you are."

I laugh softly and look up at him. "You always make me feel that way."

"And I always will."

Also by Cameron Hart

Check out my other popular series and books!
Mafia, MC, & Bodyguard Romance:
<u>Moscatelli Crime Family Series</u>[1]
<u>Di Salvo Crime Family Series</u>[2]
<u>Chaos MC series</u>[3]
<u>Savage Ride</u>[4]
Mountain Man Romance:
<u>Men of Blackthorne Mountain Series</u>[5]
<u>Bear's Tooth Mountain Men Series</u>[6]
Cowboy & Small Town Romance:
<u>Roped in by Love Series</u>[7]

---

1. https://books2read.com/u/mqBaze

2. https://books2read.com/u/m0odzW

3. https://books2read.com/u/bMVAOk

4. https://books2read.com/u/bMVlG7

5. https://books2read.com/u/3RYDvB

6. https://books2read.com/u/mVel7A

7. https://books2read.com/u/3RYlBY